The Shrouding Woman

The Shrouding Woman

Loretta Ellsworth

Henry Holt and Company
New York

For my sons Chris, Brian, and Andrew,

and my daughter Erin;

in memory of Deb Scholl Check

I would like to acknowledge Georgeanne Rundblad, professor of sociology at Illinois Wesleyan University, for providing me with her research materials on shrouding. Thanks also to Richard and Jan Graber and my first writers' group, Dave Woods, Jane Resh Thomas, and my Monday night group. I'm indebted to my exceptional agent, Jennifer Flannery, and to my editor, Christy Ottaviano, for sharing her wisdom with an inexperienced beginner. Finally, thanks to my sister Monica. Her input, as always, is priceless.

Henry Holt and Company, LLC
Publishers since 1866
115 West 18th Street, New York, New York 10011
www.henryholt.com

Henry Holt is a registered trademark of Henry Holt and Company, LLC
Copyright © 2002 by Loretta Ellsworth. All rights reserved.
Distributed in Canada by H. B. Fenn and Company Ltd.
Library of Congress Cataloging-in-Publication Data
Ellsworth, Loretta. The shrouding woman / Loretta Ellsworth. p. cm.
Summary: When her aunt Flo comes to help care for eleven-year-old Evie and her younger sister after their mother's death, Evie wants nothing to do with her and she is especially uncomfortable with her aunt's calling to help prepare bodies for burial.
[1. Aunts—Fiction 2. Death—Fiction 3. Frontier and pioneer life—Minnesota—Fiction. 4. Minnesota—Fiction.] I. Title.
PZ7.E4783 Sh 2002 [Fic]—dc21 2001039930
ISBN 0-8050-6651-9 / First Edition—2002 / Designed by Donna Mark
Printed in the United States of America on acid-free paper. ∞
3 5 7 9 10 8 6 4 2

The bustle in a house
The morning after death
Is solemnest of industries
Enacted upon earth,

The sweeping up the heart,
And putting love away
We shall not want to use again
Until eternity.

—EMILY DICKINSON

Contents

The Shrouding Woman

Papa's Sister

I was eleven years old when she came to live with us.
My little sister, Mae, was five. She came from the
western part of Minnesota, where only the hearty
survived the summer's prairie fires and the winter's
bitter cold. She traveled to our small white house on a
buckboard, her green bag caked with the dusty road.
Her dark hair was tucked under a round hat with
a short brim, and a fine netting covered her face.
Although she was Papa's sister, I'd never met her

before. All I knew about her was from a charcoal drawing of her and Papa when they were children, both with light hair and frowns upon their faces. I remembered that she was called "the Shrouding Woman" because Papa had used those words to describe her. I didn't know what it meant, but I figured it had something to do with dying. I had just lost Mama, and I didn't want to hear anything more about death, so I took Mae and hid under the front porch, peeking out through the slits in the boards between two mulberry bushes.

We heard Papa run outside; the large wooden door creaked, then slammed shut; his heavy boots shuffled on the porch above us. He helped her down from the buckboard. She clutched a Bible in one hand, and her bag was strapped over her arm.

She had the same wide nose and square shoulders as my father, but I couldn't see her eyes under the black netting. She was a tall woman, almost as tall as Papa. She gave Papa a hug and said something about what a fine woman my mama was and how she wished she'd been here to help. Papa just nodded as he carried her green bag up to the house.

"Evie and Mae, get out here," Papa called. "Come meet your aunt Flo." Mae started to move, but I shushed her still.

Mae darted a nervous glance at me. She didn't want to get a whipping, even though Papa was always soft on her.

"Don't know where they wandered off to. I guess they'll be in later." Then we heard Papa take Aunt Flo into the house.

I squeezed a fistful of dirt between my fingers. "Mama would have known we were under the porch," I said to Mae as I looked around at the piles of rocks we'd gathered to protect us against spiders.

We sat for a long time. Mae drew pictures in the dirt with a long stick, her straggly blond hair mingling with the black earth as she bent over and hummed quietly to herself. I sat in the cool darkness, watching the hot winds blow across the plains, whipping the long grass into a graceful bend.

I remembered what Mama had told me shortly before she died, her pale lips struggling with the words as I wiped her forehead. "Love your aunt Flo and make her feel welcome, Evie. She is going to take care of you and Mae for me."

The image of her lingering sickness was still fresh in my mind. Now as I sat under the porch, I thought about Mama and I wondered how I would ever live with a shrouding woman.

Aunt Flo

It was near suppertime when Mae and I went inside. I thought Papa might be angry since we were supposed to start the water boiling and bring the potatoes up from the cellar. We usually ate salt pork and dried beef throughout the winter and early spring unless Papa killed a wild turkey or a rabbit. In early June there wasn't much left in the cellar, and it would be another four weeks before we would get any bounty from our garden. When we walked in the back door, we inhaled a delicious aroma.

"Mmmm, smells like biscuits baking," Mae said as she took a deep breath.

Aunt Flo had on one of Mama's aprons, and she was stirring gravy bubbling on the stove. She stopped to wipe the perspiration off her forehead.

"Hans, please fetch me more firewood."

Papa left, whistling a happy tune with a relaxed smile on his face. He almost walked right past us, then gave me a quick wink and disappeared out the back.

Mae and I just stood there watching this odd woman, who didn't see us standing motionless near the back door. She had a large frame, unlike Mama, who used to tie the strings of the apron around her slim waist in a large bow, and even then the ends hung low. Her dark hair was piled on top of her head, making her wide face seem even more round. Two lopsided ears stuck out from the sides of her head.

I looked down at her large black shoes that were two times the size of Mama's. When she walked from the stove to the table, I noticed that her walk was clumsy and awkward.

Suddenly she turned and saw us. She stared for a long moment, and Mae pressed her back into my skirt.

"You must be Evie and Mae. I'm your aunt Flo. Mae, you've got your father's face. And Evie, you're the image of your dear departed mother." She sounded like Papa, with the same stern inflection in her voice and the thick German accent. Then she bent over and gave us a firm hug, kissing each of us on the cheek.

Her eyes seemed more welcoming than I'd imagined. I'd pictured a woman dressed in black with flaming red hair. Instead, Aunt Flo wore a blue gingham dress with a white starched collar. Her soft wrinkled flesh was warm and held a scent of witch hazel. Her green eyes reminded me of Papa. But I sensed something about her was different, and I kept a firm grip on Mae.

Aunt Flo let out a long sigh. "I wish I'd made it here before your mother died, but we only get mail once a month. I would have left earlier if I'd known she was that sick. I had to take a train to St. Paul, then a stage-coach to Winona and a buckboard from there. I didn't even get to perform her shrouding. Enough of regrets." She shook her head. "I will fix supper, and tomorrow we'll get acquainted and you can show me your farm."

She reached over to take out the dinner plates, but I pushed in front of her. "Mae sets the table," I said as I picked up the plates.

"Oh, yes. Chores are good," Aunt Flo replied. She smiled at Mae, who shyly grinned back.

Papa brought in the firewood, and Aunt Flo fixed potatoes and biscuits and creamy gravy with bits of dried beef mixed in.

"The corn is growing well for early June," Aunt Flo said to Papa as she sat down to eat. "Your crops are having a good year."

Papa nodded. "Last year we raised six hundred bushels of wheat on twenty acres along with the corn.

I'm looking to add two hundred bushels to that this year. I hired a man to work for me. I wouldn't have gotten the crops in otherwise, even though Evie was a great help near the end."

The end he spoke of was Mama's illness. Mama wanted Aunt Flo to come and live with us so we could get used to her before her time came, but Papa kept talking like Mama would recover. I fed her quinine tea for three days because her pulse was so weak, though it made her irritable. When Papa finally went to town and spent five dollars on a hat Mama had always admired, I knew her time was close. Two days later Papa spent fourteen dollars on an Atlas coffin.

"To die of consumption after God spared you all from the diphtheria," Aunt Flo said sadly.

Papa nodded. Two years earlier Minnesota had been hit with diphtheria. We felt fortunate because it passed over our house.

Papa and Aunt Flo talked well past bedtime about people I'd never heard of and the "old country" of Germany, where Aunt Flo was born. Finally Mae and

I put ourselves to bed with nobody to listen to our prayers.

I didn't sleep that night, thinking about Mama's funeral.

When Mama died, Papa sent Mae and me over to stay with our closest neighbors while two women from church came to help prepare Mama's body for burial. The next day, Mama had on her best dress. She was laid out in a casket that took up almost the whole wall of our parlor and crowded out her rocking chair. She didn't look like herself at all, not the Mama I remembered.

At the funeral, I only looked at her once, then left. I couldn't cry. All I could do was sit in the garden. The neighbors brought over lots of food and hovered over Mae and me, their eyes full of pity.

We buried Mama on a cold, rainy day. Mae skipped around Mama's grave, never understanding that she wasn't coming back, even after Papa tried to explain it to her. Two weeks later Mae cried because Mama still wasn't there to fix her hotcakes for breakfast.

Now Aunt Flo was here and Mama was gone. In our prayers that night I prayed for Mama and Mae prayed for Aunt Flo.

"Don't forget Mama," I scolded her.

"I didn't forget Mama. I just added Aunt Flo. She's going to look after us now."

"I wouldn't get too taken with her," I warned Mae.

"Why not?"

"Never you mind. We have Papa, and that's all we need. Just remember that." Then I turned away from her and grabbed all the covers.

The Wooden Box

By the next morning, Mae had forgotten what I said and was clearly taken with Aunt Flo. She was two steps behind the plump woman, following her around the kitchen like a lost kitten, showing her where everything was and acting like Aunt Flo was one of the family. She praised Aunt Flo's steamed wheat at breakfast as if it were any better than Mama's.

Later Aunt Flo braided Mae's hair and offered to make her a gingham dress. I worked on my needlepoint and cast them disapproving glances every now and then.

"What about Evie?" Mae asked, pointing to me.

"Would you like me to make you one, too?" Aunt Flo asked.

"No, thank you," I said, my voice firm. "Mama made me a green dress last year and I like it just fine." I glared at Mae as I spoke, but she was unaware of my anger. She was too busy dragging Aunt Flo outside to show her around. Mae took her down to the creek to see the crawdads, then to the garden.

I kept my distance, lingering back but still close enough to hear what they said.

"This used to be Mama's garden, but now it's Evie's," Mae said. "Evie planted it all by herself this year because Mama was sick."

"What a fine garden it is," Aunt Flo remarked somewhat loudly. "Evie must be very proud."

Mae grabbed Aunt Flo's hand. "Come, Aunt Flo. I'll show you where we go blueberrying. Last year we got almost a bushel of berries, and Papa says they should be ripe now."

That was the last straw. I sulked back to the house, hoping Mae would get the bung from the blueberries she ate.

For supper that night Aunt Flo baked a sweet bread that was her grandmother's recipe; the cinnamon aroma filled the air, and soft blueberries popped out of each piece. Papa took a deep breath when he came into the kitchen.

"Reminds me of when we were young," he said with a smile.

I ate a small bite, stuck up my nose, and made a face as I chewed. Mae and Papa finished off the rest and licked their fingers.

"Would you help me unpack?" Aunt Flo asked us after the meal.

"No," I wanted to say, but Mae was already behind her, and she wouldn't have stopped even if I'd yanked on her braid, which is what I felt like doing. How could Mae act so happy? Had she already forgotten the delicious taste of Mama's johnnycake or how Mama nursed her back to health after she ate some wild yellow sweet peas and became sick?

Mae followed Aunt Flo, but I hesitated by the door to the room that used to be mine, wishing Papa hadn't gone out to do chores.

I peeked around the door as Aunt Flo unpacked her green bag. She had hardly any clothing with her, nothing fancy or colorful. Her hair clips looked old and worn. But she placed them on the bed as if they were made from the finest porcelain. She took out a small wooden box and handed it to Mae.

"Mae, would you put this underneath the bed? Be careful with it, though. It's very special."

Mae gently placed the brown box under the bed. It was plain-looking pine with rough edges and an ill-fitting top, which looked to be homemade. I wondered what was in the box. I wondered if it had something to do with death. I wanted to reach out and grab Mae and tell her to stay away from Aunt Flo and the mysterious box.

"What else can I do to help?" Mae asked eagerly.

"You can find a spot for my lucky feather," Aunt Flo said as she handed Mae a long duck feather, with streaks of bright blue and white framed by a black tip.

"Is it really lucky?" Mae asked.

"Of course it is," Aunt Flo replied as she unpacked her clothing and placed it in Mama's bureau.

"I'll put it right here." Mae rested the feather near the front of the bureau after tickling her hands with the soft ends. She stared at the feather for a long moment. "I wish we'd had this when Mama was sick."

Aunt Flo stopped unpacking and wrapped her arms around Mae, her large body covering Mae's tiny frame.

"So do I, *mein Kind*." She spoke German like Papa did sometimes.

Mae helped Aunt Flo put the rest of her clothes in Mama's bureau, which Papa had moved into my room. I was now forced to share Mae's bed upstairs in the loft.

Aunt Flo noticed me lurking in the hallway. "Come in, Evie," she said. "Another pair of hands would be welcome."

"I can't," I said, flustered that she'd taken notice as I backed away from the door. "I have to help Papa." I turned and ran outside.

Papa was feeding the sheep in the pen next to the barn. We also had several chickens, three hogs, one cow, a draft horse, and two mares, one of which was expecting a foal. Pa had fixed a place in the barn for the occasion.

Behind the barn Crooked Creek twisted its way through our property and wound down into the valley. Even though we were a good fifteen miles away, Pa said if you listened hard enough, you could hear the mighty Mississippi roaring past. At least once a year we packed a picnic and spent the day at the state line of Minnesota, watching steamers make their way down to St. Louis and waving at Wisconsinites far away on the other side.

I walked over to the fence that ran along the pen. Several sheep came near, bleating in their teasing way, and I picked some grass to feed them. A small white lamb ran under its mother's legs, and an empty feeling came upon me.

"Papa," I called. I couldn't go inside the fence because Papa didn't trust the draft horse around us. The chestnut-colored Belgian seemed tame enough, but Papa said it didn't take much for a fifteen-hundred-pound horse to flatten a seventy-pound twig of a girl.

Papa finished filling the trough and came over to the fence.

"What is it, Evie?"

I hesitated, trying to think of how to put it. "I think Mae forgot Mama."

Papa looked down at the ground for a moment, as if he hadn't heard me. Papa always said it was his way of pondering what he was going to say. He scratched at his thinning hair. Then he looked up at me.

"Flo isn't trying to take your mama's place. Mae is just five years old. That's very young to lose a mother. It's natural she would take to Flo that way." Papa's eyes softened. "Evie, don't worry. We'll never forget your mother. You have the same golden brown hair and dimpled chin. You look just like her." He paused again. "Flo gave up a lot to come help us." He looked like he wanted to say more, but instead he returned to his work.

I wanted to stay and watch him feed the sheep. I wanted to ask him about Aunt Flo and the strange box and about her being a shrouding woman. But Papa was through with talk. He was a man of few words, and the words didn't come easily to him. Mama once told me that was the German way. Little talk and lots of hard work. I knew there was nothing left to do but pull the weeds in my garden.

The garden sat behind our house, opposite the barn and next to the prairie. Papa had built a wooden fence to keep the prairie at bay. Tall sunflowers ran along the sides of the garden so animals wouldn't nibble on our carrots. I dug my hoe into the dirt as I remembered Mama's words: "A garden is a bounty for the whole winter. You eat plenty well all year."

So we had a huge garden, with peas and squash, rutabagas, cabbage, beans, turnips, potatoes, sweet corn, and carrots. I worked alongside Mama every day in the garden, and Mae played in the dirt near the edge. Mama taught me to space the peas and how to tell when the carrots were big enough to pick.

Last year on my birthday she gave me a sketchbook.

"It's for the plants," she explained when I gave her a questioning look.

She walked to the garden and bent down low. "Look at this pea plant," she said. "Describe it, draw it, and write down everything you can about it."

So I wrote about the plants in our garden and then I studied the plants of the prairie, making sketches of them as I learned each name. Soon I could identify hundreds of plants, from the tall Indian grass that was home to the wild turkeys to the quaint thimbleweed. I could tell when bugs were eating the plants or drought was browning the edges of the leaves.

"You've learned well, Evie," Mama said after she'd taken ill. "Someday you'll teach Mae like I taught you."

I shook my head in disbelief, but Mama would have none of it.

"I'm a sensible woman," she said in the spring. "I won't see the harvest this year." Mama seemed to know her time was short long before the rest of us.

Now I looked around the garden and choked back tears. The sunflowers were growing tall again just like when Mama was here.

Searching for Twigs

Five days after Aunt Flo arrived, Papa hitched up the wagon.

"Come, Evie and Mae. We're going to Caledonia," he called out.

Mae ran to Papa, and he hoisted her up to the wagon. I was in the garden, hoping to finish weeding before the sun glared brightly. Caledonia was a bustling town with four churches, several hotels, and a general store. I dropped my hoe and brushed off my dress, smiling at the thought of a peppermint stick.

"What are you fixing to buy?" I asked.

"Some nails and stamps and a broom. Maybe a new comb for a pretty little girl," he said with a wink.

I hurried toward him.

Then I saw Papa help Aunt Flo up to the front of the wagon, and my smile vanished.

"I'm staying here to tend the garden," I called to Papa, and headed back to my work.

Papa walked over to me, his hands on his hips. "Nonsense, Evie. You spend day after day in the garden. Look at your hands. Even when you scrub them, the dirt doesn't come off. You are coming with us."

"But Papa . . ."

"Come now, Evie!" Papa rarely spoke sharply to me, so I knew I had to obey.

"Yes, Papa."

I dawdled even more as I climbed in the back of the wagon, frowning at the woman who was taking over Mama's bureau and the front of the wagon to boot.

On the road to town, Papa pointed out the landmarks along the way. We stopped at the graveyard on the hill where Mama was buried. It was the first time we'd been there since the funeral, and Mama's grave was already sprouting clover over the fresh black dirt. Mae and I decorated her plot with wild orange lilies. They were Mama's favorite. Aunt Flo bowed her head and recited several prayers in German as she rubbed Papa on the back. I watched her pray, wondering what the words meant, wondering if it had anything to do with shrouding.

Papa showed Aunt Flo where several Civil War soldiers were buried.

"We lost well over our share of men to the bloody war, all of them Union soldiers born and bred in Minnesota. Probably half of them died not from the fighting, but from the yellow fever," Papa told her. Mae and I picked some wildflowers to place on a soldier's untended grave that we decided was lonely.

Then Papa took us by a small park that had a swinging bridge extending across the narrowest part of the Winnebago River.

"A swinging bridge? Let's have our lunch there," Aunt Flo suggested. Papa pulled the wagon down onto the road winding toward the river. He stopped under a tall oak tree and tied up the horses while Mae showed Aunt Flo the way to the bridge.

"It's over yonder, Auntie Flo." She tugged on her arm, and I strolled behind them. The bridge had seemed scary the first time we crossed it, but afterward we would take turns leaning on the sides to get it to swing. Aunt Flo took a tentative step onto the bridge, hanging tightly to the top rope as she gingerly made her way across the wooden planks. Mae tried to encourage her by holding out her hand for Aunt Flo to grasp.

"Whoa," she said to the bridge as if it were a runaway horse to be calmed. "It's a mite high."

Seeing her so hesitant suddenly brought out the worst in me, and I jumped on the bridge. I made it wobble, then rocked it from side to side. Aunt Flo clung even more tightly to the rope and let out a little yelp.

"Don't scare Aunt Flo," Mae yelled at me. "She's not used to it yet, Evie."

"Sorry, Aunt Flo," I apologized, my voice almost a sneer.

Aunt Flo frowned and made her way back to the side.

"I like my feet on the ground," she said as she sank gratefully onto a bench near the bridge. "You girls go ahead. I'll watch."

I skipped across the bridge to the other side in front of Mae, who walked slowly across, looking back at Aunt Flo. By the time we made it to the other side, Mae was scowling at me.

"You scared Aunt Flo, Evie."

"Good," I replied lightly, and skipped back to the other side.

"Mean Evie," Mae called after me. "Your name is Mean Evie."

Mae's words didn't bother me, but the gentle smile on Aunt Flo's face did. I thought she'd be upset with me. I stood at the edge of the bridge, troubled by her reaction.

Papa tied up the horses and joined Aunt Flo on the bench. I worried that she would tell him what I'd done. But Aunt Flo stood up and started walking under the trees, looking at the ground.

"What are you doing, Aunt Flo?" Mae went running up to her from the bridge.

"Looking for sticks. Would you like to help me?"

Mae grabbed a long stick. "How's this one?"

"Not quite, Mae. Look for smaller sticks that have a fork in them, like this." She picked up a twig about three inches long, split at the end so it looked like a *y*.

Mae hopped along the ground, stooping to pick up sticks and examining each one carefully. Every once in a while she called out, "Here's one, Aunt Flo. This one is just right." Aunt Flo smiled at Mae, patted her on the head, and put the sticks in her pockets.

What a sight! I thought as I watched them. But when I spotted a twig with a split in it, I couldn't resist picking it up. I saw another one and picked that up, too. Soon I had a handful.

"Are we building a fire?" I asked. A slow-moving worm could melt in this heat, and I couldn't imagine what she would want a fire for.

"They're for my shrouding duties, child."

I stifled a scream and dropped a handful of forked twigs on the ground. What would dead people need with sticks?

Even Papa was now searching the ground. "Flo, I heard about a special liquid they put in the bodies of the soldiers to preserve them for the trip home during the war. Do you suppose they'll start using that on regular people when the family is far away and can't make it to the funeral quickly?"

Aunt Flo shook her head. "I can't imagine it. Anyway, they would still need someone to make the deceased presentable."

"I reckon you're right," he agreed. "It does seem strange."

Strange indeed, I thought.

Papa unpacked our picnic lunch, and I took my food up onto the bridge. I sat on the edge, sticking my feet out as if I could touch the water four feet below. I could hear Aunt Flo and Mae and Papa laughing in the cool shade while the sun burned a red spot into the part on my hair.

After lunch we stopped at the flouring mill in town, where Papa introduced Aunt Flo to everyone he met. He showed her the jail, all four churches, including the German church, and the Spettle Bakery. Mr. Spettle sold church articles as well as fine baked goods at his store. The whole town greeted Aunt Flo with open arms.

"You're fortunate to have her," Mr. Spettle told me.

We ended up at the apothecary, where Papa bought Aunt Flo special oils for her shrouding duties. I couldn't see wasting good money on oils, but I held my tongue. The new combs Mae and I got from Papa and the peppermint sticks that Mr. Frank, the grocer, gave us didn't make me feel any better.

Aunt Flo placed one hand on my shoulder and one on Mae's shoulder as she talked to Mr. Frank and watched him fetch her a bottle of oil of camphor.

"Our town is in need of your services," Mr. Frank said. "And we look forward to seeing you at the church meetings."

Aunt Flo nodded. "We'll be coming to the meetings as much as possible."

As she talked, I felt Aunt Flo's large hand press gently into my shoulder. I was reminded of the devil's claw, a sticky plant that grows on the prairie. Once it binds itself to an insect, it's impossible to get loose.

The Huckster Wagon

I fumed all the way home from town until the sight of Aunt Flo caused me physical pain.

"Papa," I called out. "I'm going to be sick." Papa pulled the wagon over and I heaved up my lunch. Papa seemed worried after that, and Aunt Flo switched spots with me so I could sit closer to him.

We barely made it home before we had a visitor. Papa was still unhitching the horse when Mr. Murdoch arrived. He was a door-to-door peddler. We enjoyed listening to his stories of back east, where people lived on top of one another, and of the West, where the Indians were still at war over the land.

Mr. Murdoch felt partial to our town, as it was named for the ancient capital of Scotland. A bagpipe, which he played on special occasions, occupied the front seat of his wagon.

"Mr. Murdoch, have you heard about the railroad coming through Caledonia?" I asked as soon as he had parked his goods in the shade.

"Indeed I have. But you'll still have need of a traveling salesman, if only to bring word that Buffalo Bill will be passing through this area next month."

"He will?" I exclaimed with wide eyes. Mr. Murdoch prided himself on bringing sensational announcements to the valley whenever he visited. Papa claimed that most of it was hearsay and not to be taken as fact, but I was always impressed.

He pulled on his thin, dark mustache as he talked. His high-pitched voice lured me to the huckster wagon, where he carried all sorts of items.

Mr. Murdoch waved his hand in the air. "Word is he's visiting a war buddy of his in Lanesboro. There's also the rumor that Sitting Bull is getting ready to surrender. Of course, with Crazy Horse shot dead, the uprisings have become less frequent."

We never had any problems with the Winnebago Indians in our area, but settlers traveling through often told of children wandering off and never being found.

Mr. Murdoch brought out a satchel. "I would kindly show you my private collection of photographs of Sitting Bull in exchange for some of that delicious steamed pudding your mother makes."

"Mama . . ." I croaked out, then stopped, unable to speak.

Mr. Murdoch took one look at my face and removed his hat. "Forgive me, lass. I'm so sorry. A more wonderful woman than your mother couldn't be found in all of Scotland."

Aunt Flo and Papa walked up behind me. She put her arms around me, and I felt myself tighten.

Papa shook the peddler's hand. "Thank you for your kind words, Mr. Murdoch. It's just a month ago we buried her, and Evie has had a hard time of it. She's feeling a bit under the weather today as well. My sister Flo is living here, and you're welcome to take supper with us all the same."

Then Papa asked him about a new spring seat for the wagon, as if that was enough talk of Mama.

Mae and Aunt Flo went to inspect the goods. Mae yearned for the pretty hair ribbons, and Aunt Flo examined spices all the way from Boston and some fancy feather dusters. Papa couldn't resist looking in a magazine that Mr. Murdoch carried with him. It had pictures of water pumps for the well.

I stood off to the side. My excitement had vanished as quickly as it had come.

"Lass, I have something I know you will envy," Mr. Murdoch said after several minutes, enticing me to come closer. I walked hesitantly toward him. Hanging from the end of the wagon were several hoes, one of which caught my attention. It had a carved wooden handle with a shiny metal blade.

"It's imported all the way from Europe," he whispered, as if it was a secret.

"It's not for people like us," I told him as I admired the carving.

"It's costly, but I've had a large share of lookers," he remarked. "It's good I have my protection," he added as he patted a rifle behind the seat. I wondered how such a lean man could shoot a big rifle like that.

Mr. Murdoch proceeded to tell us about his run-in with grasshoppers that descended upon his wagon as a thick black cloud of insects. He lay underneath the canvas until the darkened sky lightened up.

"They almost ate through the canvas. I was praying mighty hard that day."

It didn't take long to forgive Mr. Murdoch's blunder about Mama. His stories could hold my attention all night. He told us about a great fire on the prairie up in the Dakotas not far from where Aunt Flo had lived. There was also unrest with the Indians still. He finally pulled out two autographed pictures of Sitting Bull, and Mae and I stumbled over each other to get a look.

"With the new railroad coming in, it will transform the prairie forever," he predicted. "Lots of changes, now that they're giving away the land in the Dakotas to people who can prove up a homestead."

"Can anyone get a piece of land?" I asked him. I imagined a gigantic garden all my own, with mazes of vegetables.

"Anyone over the age of twenty-one. I've even seen women whose husbands died take on a homestead. One woman sixty years old came out from Pennsylvania to homestead near her sons. Of course, most Christian men disapprove of women in the fields. It's a hard living, and many of them have sod homes, not wooden ones."

I frowned at his comment. Papa was a good Christian, and he didn't disapprove of my garden.

Aunt Flo made supper while Mr. Murdoch continued to entertain us. I left to fetch the water from the
well and peel potatoes, then hurried back to hear him
talk. He was full of tales from the big city, where
houses sat inches apart from one another, something I
couldn't imagine since our nearest neighbor was over
a mile away.

"A wonderful Yankee dinner," he complimented
Aunt Flo. "Vegetables and meat and bread. Seems
cheese is all I eat on the other side of the Mississippi."

Dinner went well until he found out about Aunt
Flo being a shrouding woman. He made some unfa-
vorable comments that upset her awful.

"Those informal folkways are changing," he began.
"I've seen some fine funeral homes starting up in the
cities. Word is that every town will soon have one."

Aunt Flo's eyes narrowed. "Are you saying they
can do a better job than someone who has been
trained by her ancestors? Better than the tradition
that is learned from one generation to the next?"

Mr. Murdoch nodded, and his thin mustache twitched. "Only telling what I've heard."

Aunt Flo's reply was a simple "Hmph!" I could sense she wanted to say more but was holding back.

"There's a new science of embalming," he continued. "Shrouding is becoming a thing of the past."

Aunt Flo stuck out her bulky hands. "No science can replace this. The touch of human skin on human skin," she said loudly.

Mr. Murdoch straightened up in his chair. He seemed taken aback by Aunt Flo's words. "Times are changing," he muttered, almost to himself.

Aunt Flo went straight to her room after Mr. Murdoch left without buying any of the spices that she'd been tempted to purchase beforehand.

I didn't understand Aunt Flo, and I couldn't fathom why she used special oils like camphor or what was in the old brown box underneath her bed. Besides, something Aunt Flo said bothered me. She told Mr. Murdoch that shrouding was a tradition learned from one generation to the next. Aunt Flo had no children, so the next generation would be Mae and me. Neither Papa nor Aunt Flo mentioned any notions they might have on this subject.

Still, the idea worried me as I helped Papa with clover cutting the next day. It worried me as I gathered eggs and applied goose grease to our mare's sore leg. I determined to watch this strange woman who was unlike anyone I'd ever met before. I would watch her carefully and learn more about this business of shrouding. Then I would talk to Papa.

The Storm

I stood at the edge of the garden, peering at two long weeds dangling beside a cornstalk. The rest of the garden was meticulously weeded, and after recent rains it bore lavish green leaves and luscious, ripe vegetables. Papa never worked on Sundays, even if it rained the entire week and he sorely needed to get in the fields. I wasn't allowed to work in the garden on Sundays, either, although I was tempted to pick a ripe ear of corn every now and then.

Even though we didn't make it to church meetings very often, we always spent Sunday in a Christian manner. Papa or Mama would read Scripture from the Bible, and Mae and I practiced our prayers so that when we did make it to church, we wouldn't be lacking. On hot summer Sundays, we often picnicked down at the creek. Mae and I would wade in the water as we looked for toads underneath the rocks.

"I wonder if Aunt Flo is a Christian?" I asked Mae this Sunday morning.

Mae looked thoughtful as she picked dandelions. "Do Christians say prayers?"

"Of course they do," I replied.

"Aunt Flo says prayers at dinner, doesn't she?"

"Yes, but they're in German," I objected. "We don't know what she's saying."

"Is Papa a Christian?" Mae asked, her hands turning a yellow shade from the petals.

"Of course he is."

"Papa speaks German," Mae said.

"I suppose Papa wouldn't let Aunt Flo say un-Christian prayers at our table," I conceded, not thoroughly convinced.

Unless she cast a spell on him, I thought. Last year when the circus came through, I saw a man who mixed potions and spells and sold them in a bottle. Maybe Aunt Flo had a spell that worked on everybody except me. Why else would they all like her so much?

We sorely needed rain, and judging by the way Papa's leg bothered him, he said we were in for a big storm. After Papa had read from the Bible and we recited our prayers, Aunt Flo packed a picnic lunch. Just as soon as we settled down by the creek, the sky turned purple. It became as dark as night, and the clouds moved swiftly over our heads. Papa was sure it was a sign of a twister.

He grabbed the picnic lunch, and Aunt Flo scooped up Mae. We all ran back to the house. The skies opened on us in full force, soaking us right to the skin. With the rain came the wind, strong at first, dying down briefly, and then coming back with a fury.

Papa had to yank hard to open the cellar door.

"Evie, you take Mae and Aunt Flo and light the candles down there. I'll be back as soon as I take care of the animals."

"I want to come with you," I hollered, but Papa shook his head, pushed me toward the stairs, and closed the door above us.

"Papa!"

"Everything will be fine, Evie," I heard a voice say in the darkness. "Help me find the candles."

I groped, following the walls, until I found the candles and a match to light them. The candles cast a shadow across the cellar, where Mama's supply of beans and watermelon pickles and corn was stored. A spider ran across the wall, casting a monstrous shadow in the faint light. Aunt Flo turned two bean pails over to use as chairs.

I wondered if the twister had followed her here, bringing death in its path to give her more work.

The howling wind grew louder above us, and Mae hid her face in Aunt Flo's skirt. We were wet and cold and afraid.

"Is Papa going to die?" Mae cried.

Aunt Flo hugged Mae against her wet skirt. "Of course not. We must be brave and help your father."

"How can we help? He won't let us," I said. Tears trickled down my cheeks.

"You can still help. You can pray together for his safe return. You girls recite your prayers. Now stop that crying, both of you," she gently scolded us.

I wiped away the tears and tried to remember the prayers I had just said that morning, but the door above pounded as though the wind was trying to reach down into the cellar and swallow us up. No words or Scripture came to mind. Mae just stared at the door, too scared to speak.

Finally Aunt Flo started to recite a prayer. It was my mother's favorite Scripture passage from St. John about loving one another and keeping the commandments. She spoke softly and covered my shaking hands with hers, and soon I found my voice and prayed with her, nodding at Mae to do the same. Aunt Flo's low voice blended with ours.

In a short while the noise above us became a distant sound. Then we heard a loud creak and looked up to see Papa opening the cellar door. The sky above him was light again.

"Papa!" Mae and I ran up the stairs and grabbed him around the waist.

"Papa, you didn't blow away!" Mae yelled. Papa hugged us both, something he hadn't done much in a while.

"I saw a cloud dip down into the fields, so I stayed in the barn while it blew by. It's past us now. Be thankful it didn't blow down our house or barn."

"We prayed for you, Papa. Aunt Flo helped us," Mae said.

"And good prayers they were," Aunt Flo added.

"Look." Papa pointed to fallen tree limbs scattered on the ground, one limb barely missing the back of our house. "We were fortunate today."

Our house and barn and livestock were intact. The crops were ravaged in one area, but the rest remained unharmed, as though the twister had purposely picked one spot in the middle of the field to destroy. The wooden fence that ran along our property was broken apart, and chunks of wood dotted the prairie grass.

Then I saw Mama's garden. I gasped at the sight. It was torn apart, covered in mud. Only a few plants remained, and they looked flattened. The rest of the garden was reduced to rubble.

"Evie, look!" Mae exclaimed when she saw it.

"Maybe it can still be saved," Papa said as he walked around the edge, examining the damage.

"I'm so sorry about your garden," Aunt Flo said, putting her hand on my shoulder. "We'll help you save what's left."

"It's not my garden," I replied, my voice cracking. "It's Mama's garden. She wanted *me* to take care of it."

"Are you sure you don't want help? There's a lot of work here," Papa said.

"I'll do it myself," I insisted, feeling my throat catch on the last word, turning from Aunt Flo so she wouldn't see me all choked up. "I'll start tomorrow."

Papa shrugged and looked at Aunt Flo.

"If that's what you want. I have some work to do as well," Papa remarked as he looked at the broken fence, the fallen limbs, and the scattered leaves covering the yard and part of the field. Mae and I went into the house, but Aunt Flo didn't follow. A short while later she still hadn't come in, so we set out to look for her.

"There she is," Mae yelled, pointing toward the field. Aunt Flo was working next to Papa with a scythe, chopping away at the storm's messy remains.

"She's working on the Lord's Day," Mae protested.

"So is Papa," I reminded her. I pulled on Mae's arm. "Come with me," I commanded her. Mae and I set to work gathering the broken limbs into a big pile.

"I guess Aunt Flo's not an old gooseberry," I said as I dragged a large branch across the yard.

"What's a gooseberry?" Mae asked.

"Someone who knows evil magic and casts spells."

Mae put her hands on her hips. "Of course she's not. She helped me fix a baby robin's wing and held me on her shoulders while I put it back in the nest. Not even Mama would do that. Mama always said, 'Nature has a way of caring for her own.'"

"Mama was just being practical," I said as I threw the branch into the pile. "There are things about Aunt Flo you don't understand. She's . . . peculiar," I said as I searched for a way to explain it to her.

Mae nodded in agreement. "She's nice. She gives good hugs."

I shook my head. Mae couldn't possibly understand. Aunt Flo was different. She gathered us into her huge arms and gave us bear hugs every morning when we got up and in the evening before bed. She traipsed around catching butterflies with Mae in the middle of the day. She was outspoken and didn't care who knew it.

I wasn't superstitious like Mrs. Finn, who believed that a white moth inside the house meant death and who said that if a dog howled at night when there's illness in the house, it was a bad omen.

But I feared Aunt Flo and her strange profession. Papa and Aunt Flo had talked about shrouding like it was as natural as a sheep giving birth. Mae had no inkling what shrouding was. I didn't understand it, but I knew that nothing good came from death and nothing good could come from a woman who dealt in death. And I prayed Aunt Flo would never be called upon in the Crooked Creek Valley.

The Funeral

It was late on a Thursday evening when we heard the sound of horses pulling a rackety wagon out front. It was a humid night, the kind where damp hair clung to the back of my neck and my clammy feet stuck to the wooden floor. Papa feared another storm might be brewing, and we hadn't finished cleaning up from the last one. Mama's garden was still a wreck. The plants I'd saved were mostly the ones that grew under-ground, like the potatoes and carrots.

We sat in the parlor, fanning ourselves, protected

from the mosquitoes but too hot to sleep. We heard footsteps on the porch and a soft knock. Papa opened the wooden door to find Mr. Severson standing with his son, Edward.

They lived on the winding creek to the south of our farm. Their family had been one of the first to set up a homestead in the Crooked Creek Valley. Papa said that Mr. Severson had been only a baby when his family left Norway.

Mr. Severson looked past Papa into the room where Aunt Flo sat with Mae on her lap. Aunt Flo stiffened and looked up.

"Evening, Hans," he said softly to Papa, who invited them into the parlor.

"How is your father doing?" Papa asked. Mr. Severson's father had been sick for a long time.

"He passed away a couple of hours ago," Mr. Severson said, his head down, his hand on his son's shoulder. "I knew your sister was here, and we wondered if she would mind preparing him for burial. We heard she performs shroudings."

Papa looked at Aunt Flo, who nodded. "She'd be honored," Papa said.

My mouth flew open, and I shuddered as if a sudden chill had crept upon me. Aunt Flo got up, and I followed her down the hallway. She disappeared into her bedroom. I peeked around the door, holding my breath so she wouldn't hear me. She opened her drawer and took out a shawl. Then she went to her bed, knelt down, and pulled out the wooden box from underneath.

I wondered if it was full of those forked twigs and strange ointments. I moved as I heard Aunt Flo coming out of her room. She stopped short when she saw me.

"Evie, you gave me a fright." Then she noticed me staring at the box. "Are you all right?"

"I'm—I'm fine," I stuttered, backing away.

"Take care of your sister this evening," she said as she wrapped an arm around me and gave me a quick embrace. I flinched as the box rubbed up against my waist.

"I have my buckboard out front," Mr. Severson said as Aunt Flo put on her shawl and followed him out the door. We soon heard the sound of horses galloping down the road.

"Where is Aunt Flo going?" Mae asked Papa, her eyes wide and troubled.

Papa answered her in a calm voice. "She went to help the Seversons. She'll be back soon. You both get to bed now." He picked up Mae and carried her upside down over his shoulder so that she squealed with delight. Then he picked me up and put me over his other shoulder. I giggled, too. I didn't care if I was too big for such things. It was nice to have Papa close again, even just for a minute.

I tried to stay awake, the image of Aunt Flo's mysterious box floating in my mind. I could see Mama laid out in her coffin in the middle of our parlor. Well-meaning words of comfort faded behind me. "God's timing is best" and "Heaven is a better place."

I had sought Mama's presence in the garden. I wanted her to live even when I saw the pain in her face, even when Papa said it was best for her to go so she wouldn't suffer any longer. I had whispered my sins into the cold spring wind ripping through the garden.

Papa sat up late, waiting for Aunt Flo to return, and the light from the lantern flickered in our room, dancing up the walls to form strange shapes. Mae was next to me, breathing softly, her body curved in a small ball, her back pressing against mine. The light was still there when I finally fell off to sleep.

When I awoke the next morning, Papa was gone and Aunt Flo was in the kitchen, humming as if nothing had happened. The air felt cool and not as sticky. Mae was already outside, running up and down the slanted cellar door.

"Where's Papa?" I asked, rubbing the sleep from my eyes.

"He left hours ago for the fields. You slept late this morning, Evie. You must have been tired."

"I was waiting up for you." Then I quickly added, "I didn't want Papa to be worried."

Aunt Flo stopped stirring the custard she was making and turned to look at me. I saw a little smile at the corner of her mouth.

"That was nice of you, Evie."

My face grew hot and red. Then I saw the wooden box sitting on the table. I stared, wanting to ask her about it, wondering if I should.

Aunt Flo spoke before I could ask. "Evie, would you place my box underneath my bed and put on your good dress? We're going to pay our respects to the Severson family."

Ever so slowly I picked up the brown box. Whatever was inside was moving around. I kept it at arm's length. I felt Aunt Flo's eyes on me, so I walked quickly to her room and slid the box underneath her bed. Then I ran to the washroom and scrubbed my hands till they were pink.

Aunt Flo fixed a custard dessert and took a jar of watermelon pickles that Mama had made last year.

Papa hitched up the wagon, and we rode to the Severson farm. Mr. Severson was a grumpy old man with a white beard who always wore the same plaid shirt, except in the summer. He didn't speak English well and usually muttered in Norwegian. Still, Edward often talked about fishing with his grandfather, and he seemed to enjoy him. Old Mr. Severson always had a Bible in one hand and a fishing pole in the other, and I sometimes wondered if he quoted Scripture to the fish to lure them close to shore.

When we pulled into the Severson farm, Edward was out front, throwing stones at a tree. He had the same blond hair and light complexion as his father. His cheeks were turning pink from the bright sun. Papa put his hand on Edward's shoulder.

"How's the wheat doing?" he asked Edward.

I gripped Mae's hand tightly as we entered the house. The air inside smelled of musty garments. Mae and I stayed near the door. An uncomfortable feeling settled in my stomach when I saw the body. Mr. Severson was laid out in a casket in the parlor with a fresh bouquet of daisies at his feet. He was wearing a clean white shirt and a bow tie. His hair was combed neatly for a change, and he had a small Bible in his hands. He looked like he was sleeping, except that his mouth hung slightly open, and he didn't have his usual grumpy look anymore.

The Seversons had a small family service with a few neighbors but no pastor since they weren't very churched in the traditional manner. Everyone gathered around the casket. Mae grabbed Aunt Flo's hand, and I stood behind Papa. Mae kept peeking around Aunt Flo's skirt, as if she didn't quite understand the seriousness of the event. Edward's father read a psalm from the Bible and talked about how his father brought him over as a boy to America. Edward's mother dabbed at her puffy eyes every once in a while. I heard her tell Aunt Flo that she stayed up all night to watch over Mr. Severson.

Why did she stay up all night? I thought. *He's already dead.*

Soon after, I took Mae outside and we walked over to a brook near their farm to watch the crawdads splash back and forth. Mae clapped and giggled at their movements, but I kept her from catching them so her dress would stay clean. A slow procession carried the casket up a steep hill to the Seversons' burial plot. We saw the people gathered at the top of the hill as they lowered Mr. Severson's covered casket into the ground. It was next to a cross, where his wife was buried. Then Mrs. Severson led the people in singing "Blest Be the Tie That Binds" before going back inside.

Later I saw Edward outside again, throwing rocks at the tree. I didn't know what to say, so I joined him and threw rocks alongside him. Mae picked up some and threw them, too, missing the tree completely.

"Are you going to be a shrouding woman?" Edward suddenly asked me.

I stopped my throw, my hand suspended in midair. "Why do you ask that?"

He kept throwing rocks as he talked. "Well, your aunt told my pa that she came from a long line of shrouding women. I figured you might be one, too."

"You must be mistaken," I replied.

"Maybe when you grow up . . ."

I stuck my chin in the air and folded my arms. "I don't know anything about shrouding, but I'm sure I would know if a custom was being passed down to me or not," I replied more primly than I had intended.

He shrugged and continued pitching stones at the tree while Mae imitated him. I stopped throwing rocks and sat on the porch. Edward acted as though he didn't believe me. I had known Edward my whole life. We'd studied geography together, and feelings ran high between us during spelling competitions. We'd even suffered together with a terrible bout of dysentery after swimming in the old creek. How could Edward mistake me as taking part in the strange tradition of my aunt?

But what if Edward was right? Was I destined to grow up to be like Aunt Flo, bringing out my wooden box in the middle of the night? Was I doomed to follow in her footsteps?

I walked over to the corner of the house, where Mrs. Severson had stored several ginseng plants in the shade of a maple tree after making a medicinal tea for Edward's grandfather. I examined the whitish yellow root, remembering all I'd learned from Mama. Ginseng is a perennial, dying down in the fall and reviving in the spring. A scar is left just above the root each time the plant dies off.

If the Crooked Creek Valley was a ginseng plant and each time a person died it added a scar, then our part of the country would have seen enough loss to make a twenty-foot-long ginseng root.

There would always be customers for Aunt Flo's business. But tradition or not, I couldn't bear the thought of hanging around death's door for the rest of my life.

It was time to talk to Papa.

The Fox

I tried to find Papa alone, but when I approached him in the barn, our mare Daisy picked the same moment to deliver her foal.

"Run and get the goose grease," Papa ordered. When Mae and Aunt Flo found out what I needed, they came following to watch the birthing.

"I don't think Mama would like Mae watching this," I told Aunt Flo, hoping she'd take Mae back inside so I could talk to Papa alone.

"Mama let me see a lamb born last year," Mae protested.

"Don't see how this will harm her," Aunt Flo said. "I'll keep her out of the way."

Less than an hour later a beautiful brown foal was born in the barn. Mae named her Clover because Daisy loved the clover Mae fed her often.

I tried to talk to Papa the next day after he'd put up a load of wheat and hitched the horse to the wagon, but Aunt Flo showed up to bring Papa a drink of water and a sandwich.

"Thank you, Flo. You saved me a trip inside," Papa replied as he guzzled down the water. Then he climbed into the wagon. "I'll be back as soon as I take this wheat to the mill."

"Can I come with you, Papa?" I asked.

Papa shook his head. "Flo needs you to lend a hand making soap. I'll help when I get back. Maybe we'll make enough soap to last through the winter."

Then he yelled, "Giddyap," and was gone.

I groaned. I hated making soap in the summer because it was a hot task and it took such a long time.

Aunt Flo linked her arm through mine. "Evie, if you find some fragrant flower petals, I'll add oatmeal and make a perfumed soap. We can save it for special occasions."

The quest for fragrant flower petals was an opportunity to get away from Aunt Flo and soap making for a while. I wandered off into the prairie, searching for goldenrod or purple coneflower. The tall grass encircled the knee-high corn, bordering it like a picture frame. I stayed near the edge, aware of how easily a person could get lost in the thick, green-and-gold brush strokes of the prairie grass. I meandered as if I had the entire day, looking for just the right flowers, skipping over the common milkweed and steering clear of badger holes.

I saw the newly opened black-eyed Susan scattered among the white spires of baptisia, a harvest of colors and sweet smells that wove endlessly through the prairie. I pushed away a towering compass plant and had taken a step when I heard a piercing cry below.

I screamed and jumped. There at my feet was a baby fox, cowering in a small ball of fear.

"What are you doing all alone out here, little friend?" I bent down, and the pup let out a loud squeak and stared at me with wide eyes.

"It's all right," I said soothingly. I looked for signs of a mother fox hiding in the tall brush but found none. I thought of what Mama would say.

"If you touch a wild animal, the mother will smell you and reject her baby," she'd warned me on several occasions.

"I'd like to help, but it's best I leave you."

The pup continued to stare at me, and I noticed a white spot on the tip of one of its black ears. Its rust-colored coat blended into the prairie. I backed up behind the compass plants, watching the fox, hoping to see it walk away. It didn't move. I stepped farther back, sat down in the prairie grass, and waited.

I looked up at the sun, which was now straight above me. I had been gone too long already. I pulled the stems off the thimbleweed plants that grew down among the grasses and played "He loves me not." I could barely see the pup through the brush. It shifted every now and then but didn't stand.

I thought of Aunt Flo mending a bird's injured wing and helping Mae place it back in the nest. Would she scold me for bringing home an abandoned baby fox?

The Indian grass crinkled to my left, and I looked up to see a big muskrat slinking along the brush, its wide jaw open. It was headed straight toward the pup. I jumped at once.

"Scoot!" I screamed as loud as I could. The frightened muskrat turned and ran in the opposite direction.

I walked back to the pup, reached down, and picked it up. It let out another cry and squirmed its black feet against my hands. I wrapped it tightly in my apron and headed home.

I passed Mama's garden, still struggling to recover from the early summer storm. Mae was sitting on the cellar door. She ran to meet me, her brows narrowed down toward angry eyes.

"Where have you been, Evie?"

"It's no concern of yours," I replied as I went around her.

"Aunt Flo is boiling the fat in the kettle and needs someone to pour the lye while she stirs. You were supposed to be back long ago," Mae yelled behind me.

I stopped in my tracks.

"This is why I'm late," I said, and showed her the bundle in my apron.

"Ooh," she said, and nodded approvingly. "Are you going to keep it?"

"If Papa lets me."

"What about Aunt Flo? Aren't you going to ask her first?"

"Aunt Flo doesn't need to know about this yet. I'll fix a spot in the barn until I can come back later and figure out how to feed it. I'll ask Papa when he gets home."

"But Aunt Flo could help," Mae whined.

"No," I insisted. "What Aunt Flo doesn't know won't hurt her. Now promise you won't tell."

Mae made a cross on her chest with her finger, our sign for heavenly promises.

"Good. Follow me," I commanded as I walked to the barn and secured a safe area with a small amount of leftover fencing to keep the fox in. I set the soft creature down on some straw. It stood for a moment as if it didn't know what to do, then ran to the corner and hid.

"Keep an eye on it so it doesn't get away," I told Mae before I went to the house.

The heat from the stove hit me as soon as I opened the door. Aunt Flo was stirring the mixture in the large kettle.

My job was to break the cooled soap into bars and set it out to dry in the sun. After they dried, I would store the bars in a box. The hardest part was pouring the mixture from the hot kettle into the cooling tub, which was why Papa usually helped make soap.

Aunt Flo turned and saw me. Drops of sweat ran down the sides of her face. She looked puzzled.

"Evie, where are the flower petals?"

I looked down at my empty hands.

Making Soap

"I didn't find any petals," I mumbled sheepishly.

Aunt Flo straightened up and put her hands on her hips. "We will talk about this when your father gets back. Go outside and check the soap."

There was a tub already cooling in the sun. I ran a knife through the soap; it was still soft.

I took an old bowl from the cellar, filled it with water from the well, and brought it into the barn, where Mae was trying her best to pick up the baby fox while it bit at her hand.

"Let it be," I yelled at her. "Here's some water. Maybe it will take a drink if you haven't frightened it too much already." I put the water down, and Mae scooted the fox over until it fell into the water bowl.

"Be careful, Mae."

The fox jumped out and ran to the corner again.

"Where did you find it?" Mae asked.

"On the prairie. It was almost a meal for a muskrat."

"He's lucky you saved him. That's what his name should be. Lucky."

"Lucky," I tried the name out, and agreed.

"He's awful skinny," Mae noted.

"He's probably an orphan." Mae had already decided it was a boy.

"What do you feed a fox?"

"I'm not sure. Maybe scraps from the table," I suggested.

A loud voice startled us both. "Evie, what are you doing in the barn?" I turned to see Aunt Flo behind me, a look of exasperation on her face. "You disappear quicker than whiskey at a wedding dance."

Mae moved aside, and Aunt Flo saw the fox. "So this is what you've been up to." She bent down and examined the pup.

"You shouldn't take a wild animal away from its home, Evie." Her voice was stern, and I was certain she was going to make me take it back to the prairie.

My voice squeaked. "It was orphaned. I waited for the mother to return, but she never did."

Silence filled the barn. Mae and I looked at each other, waiting for Lucky's sentence.

Aunt Flo stood up. "You will feed it here for two weeks. Any longer and it won't be able to return to the wild. Give it hard-boiled eggs, fruit, bread, and water. After that you can leave food for it at the edge of the prairie every day for another two weeks. Then it will be on its own, able to survive."

"What if the badgers eat its food?" I objected. Badgers were known scavengers of the prairie.

"You can put blueberries around the edge. The badgers have a sweet tooth and will eat the fruit and leave the other food alone."

I thought about waiting to talk to Papa. But in my gut I knew how Papa felt about wild animals when he had livestock to be concerned about. Finally I stood and faced Aunt Flo. "All right," I conceded. I turned to Mae. "At least Lucky will have a chance this way."

"That's settled, then," Aunt Flo said. "Now come help me add the lye before the fat hardens and the soap is ruined."

"I'll get some bread and fruit for Lucky," Mae said.

I followed Aunt Flo into the house. I wasn't happy with her decision, but I wasn't about to argue for fear that she'd make me turn Lucky out right then and there. I also knew Papa would go along with whatever Aunt Flo decided.

I worked hard the rest of the day. I brought up the bucket of fat cracklings from the cellar. Aunt Flo added the lye, and I stirred the cracklings in the big copper kettle and removed any meat I found, making it smooth and clean. I kept stirring until it left a creamy glop on the spoon.

Aunt Flo touched the spoon to her tongue. "It's done," she announced when she decided it had the right taste. We both heaved the kettle over to the waiting pans and emptied the contents. Then we started all over again.

Papa returned and helped us with the soap making. There were several times when we were alone and I could have talked to him about Aunt Flo, but I chose not to. The urgency I'd felt before had dissolved into a nagging worry, like a thorn just beneath the skin.

Besides, Aunt Flo hadn't mentioned my long absence to Papa, and I didn't want to give her cause to bring it up. I also didn't want to ruin my time with Papa in an argument or a lecture on responsibility. Lately he'd taken to getting up earlier and working later, as if hard work was his only comfort. I had grown used to hearing his heavy footsteps on the floor of the parlor and the squeak of the rocking chair that he resorted to in the middle of the night when he couldn't sleep.

Mama's rocking chair, I thought as I recalled the evenings spent with Mama crocheting in her chair while Mae played at her feet.

Over the next two weeks I didn't complain much about anything, even when Aunt Flo made me rework my stitches in the mourning picture I had embroidered for Mama. I had started it the week after Mama died but kept putting it down. Finally it was finished: a garden of white lilies accented with a yellow monarch butterfly. I set Mama's tombstone in the back with her full name across it. But Aunt Flo took one look at the back, where threads hung down and crossed over large spaces, and made me redo the butterfly. She said the back ought to be as neat as the front and suggested that if I wanted to hang it in the parlor, I should show my best work.

I tore out the stitches even though I didn't think Mama would mind a few loose ends.

That same day Aunt Flo made good on her word and had us turn Lucky loose.

"It's been fourteen days," she reminded me. Mae and I reluctantly took Lucky to the edge of the prairie and fed him the last meal we would be able to watch him eat. Mae whimpered that she'd miss Lucky even though he still bit at her fingers when she reached for him. I shuddered at the thought of what might become of a small fox alone on the prairie.

Finally we ran home. Lucky followed at first but couldn't keep up, and that was the last we saw of him.

For two more weeks we left food at the same spot each night, and by early morning it had disappeared. Several days later I thought I caught a glimpse of Lucky. I snuck to the spot and left food scraps, but Aunt Flo saw me.

She reminded me of our agreement.

"That fox will never make it through the winter if you don't let him survive on his own." She added, "He has to learn to hunt for his food."

I knew Aunt Flo was right about Lucky, but her hard lessons didn't endear her to me.

On Sunday before the church meeting, Reverend Johanson and the whole community paid Aunt Flo a special honor. They'd heard about her laying out Mr. Severson, and everyone complimented her on doing such a fine job. Aunt Flo was bewildered by all the attention but acted polite enough.

"Back on the homestead I wasn't used to talking to more than two people a week," she said. "I'm a bit flustered." I didn't understand why, but that seemed to make everyone like her even more.

Reverend Johanson looked right at me as he filled the church with his booming voice. "Summer is a time to move ahead and reap new life and leave our burdens behind," he said with divine inspiration.

I wanted to believe him, but the thought of Mama still turned my heart upside down.

The Custom

It seemed as if Aunt Flo had taken over our entire household by the middle of summer. What's more, she didn't act a bit neighborly like Mama did. She was friendly enough when Edward's mother came to visit, but she outright told her that she didn't have time to sit and chat much, and especially didn't like gossip, which sent Edward's mother off in quite a huff.

I worked this matter into a conversation with Papa, but it went right over his head as though it wasn't the terrible thing that it really was. Papa shrugged and said, "That's just Flo's way."

Then there was the matter of Mama's butter churn, which had been a wedding present. Aunt Flo used it to make honey butter.

"Mama always makes it plain," I told her.

Aunt Flo smiled, handed me a slice of bread, and nudged my shoulder. "Give this butter a try. I'm sure you'll love it as much as I do, Evie."

I put the bread down. "Do you expect me to like all your traditions?"

Aunt Flo looked confused. "Are you talking about butter?"

I shook my head. "I don't want to talk about it." I went to Mama's garden, where I curled myself up beneath the cornstalks. It wasn't the butter that bothered me so much. It was the memory of making the butter with Mama. Mae would add the cream while I turned it over, then we poured off the frothy buttermilk into waiting cups and sprinkled salt on the hardened butter. Afterward we clinked our cups together and toasted our good fortune.

Aunt Flo hadn't even asked us to help make the butter. That night I emptied the churn when no one was watching.

The next morning Aunt Flo was plumb befuddled by the empty churn and butter on the floor.

"How did this happen?" she asked.

Papa looked at me, his eyebrows raised in suspicion.

I shrugged. "I think I saw Mae playing around it. She probably knocked it over. You know how careless she can be."

"I did not do it!" Mae protested.

"You might not have meant to do it," I added, "but accidents happen to little girls who run in the house."

My comment set Mae to bawling inconsolably until Papa finally sent her to the loft. Later I felt so guilty that I snuck her a piece of bread and jam. Good old Mae was used to my mean streaks and forgave me on the spot.

The following day, Aunt Flo came out to the garden as I dug up the weeds crowding the flowers. The hearty daylily was one of the few flowers that had survived and was in full bloom, in a dazzling combination of orange, yellow, and pink. I had hopes for the squash, but most of the garden was limp.

"I'm sorry, Mama," I whispered to the withered cabbage plants that were failing despite my best efforts. Some days I felt as if I could look up and see her working across from me, bending low over the rows of beans in the flowered bonnet that she always wore to fend off the morning sun. But as soon as my mind convinced itself that she was there, I would look up and the vision would vanish and I'd be left alone again.

"You are doing a fine job on your garden, Evie," Aunt Flo called out. She carried wild daisies in her apron to make into a hair band for Mae. She twirled the stems together as she spoke.

"It's a sight," I replied as I glanced at her, then returned to my task of pulling weeds. "The leaves on the green beans are brown, and the squash aren't any bigger than peas. Besides, it isn't my garden."

"You take good care of it. Perhaps now the garden will be yours." I looked up at her. She stood near the edge, as though she wanted to come in and help but was waiting for an invitation. Her face held a wistful expression as she fluffed the white petals. It wasn't in my nature today to be kind back.

"I don't want it to be mine. It belongs to Mama."

"You have your mother's looks, but your father's disposition." Aunt Flo laughed. "In the old country, we hand down to our children our belongings and our land. It is our custom."

I stopped pulling weeds and looked up. "Is it a custom to be a shrouding woman?"

"Yes." Aunt Flo nodded as she twisted the green stems. "My mother was a shrouding woman, as well as her mother before her. I learned when I was young, like you, and have been doing it most of my life."

I cringed at the thought.

Aunt Flo seemed to sense my concern. "What is it, Evie? Is something bothering you?"

I stood up, dropping a handful of weeds. The words were forming, although I was afraid to hear the answer. It squeaked out on its own. "And who will you pass the custom down to?"

Aunt Flo tilted her head in a thoughtful manner. "I was married once. We built a homestead in the Dakotas and planned to raise a large family, but my husband died." She smiled sadly. "We didn't have children. I guess it will end with me."

I let out a huge sigh of relief. "If you had a child, would she become a shrouding woman?"

Aunt Flo looked down at the flowers. "I don't know. It's not something I think about. Perhaps."

"You don't expect it of anyone? It is a choice?" I asked to be certain.

She looked back up at me, the corners of her

mouth firm. "Shrouding isn't for everyone. Only those who are called to the profession."

I raised my eyebrows in disbelief.

Aunt Flo twirled the delicate flower stems together. "A shrouding woman's profession is a noble one," she said, her voice lighter than before. "She is the care-taker of the dead, preparing them for burial, provid-ing her service to the family of the deceased."

I wiped my hands on my apron, smearing it with a green stain. I was possessed with a sudden curiosity I hadn't felt before. "How do you prepare them for burial?"

"I give them a look of peace." She sounded pleased, and a gentle smile touched her lips.

"Do you enjoy doing it?" I blurted out, unable to stop myself.

"It is something I take pride in doing, just like you are proud of your garden."

I stuck my hands into the dirt, feeling the coolness of the black soil.

"Mama said the soil gives life," I replied.

Aunt Flo held up a perfectly round green-and-white hair band dotted with yellow specks. "That is true. It is also where we bury the dead."

I looked down at the soil and drew my hands out of the dirt.

Aunt Flo stepped forward, still careful not to enter the garden. "Perhaps someday you will understand it, Evie."

I shook my head.

"My ways are different, but if it bothers you, I will not talk about it." She stopped, then added, "And I will only make plain butter from now on."

My face reddened. She knew all along that it was me who knocked over the churn. I wondered why she didn't tell on me. "You would make plain butter?" I asked instead.

Aunt Flo nodded. "For you, yes."

"Can Mae and I help?" I asked timidly.

"Of course," she replied eagerly. Aunt Flo's eyes swept across the garden.

"Shall we make a cake for our supper?" she asked, pointing to the ripe carrots that were half the size of last year's crop.

"Mama loved carrot cake," I responded, and I smiled for the first time in a long while.

Carrot Cake

Aunt Flo and I spent the rest of the afternoon making a carrot cake to go with dinner. I chopped the vegetables and simmered them on the stove until they were soft while Aunt Flo mashed the boiled potatoes for the corn hash. While we worked, Aunt Flo reminisced about Mama.

"I met your mother when she and Hans were newlyweds. She was a very good cook even though she was young. You are a good cook, too, Evie. That is something your mother gave you."

Carrot Cake

"She did teach me to make this cake," I admitted as I added a pinch of cinnamon just how Mama showed me. "And she taught me the best way to scrub clothes and how to care for bee stings."

"She also gave you a love of gardening," Aunt Flo reminded me.

"Yes," I replied. "Mama always declared that the fruits of our labor are sweeter on our tongues."

"How true," Aunt Flo said.

"Except for this year." I sighed as I chopped a pitiful-looking carrot. "I'd hoped the garden would be more plentiful."

"Don't give up, Evie. The year isn't over yet. There are many weeks of sunshine and warmth still left."

Aunt Flo added cold meat to the hash and made patties, which she dipped in flour and fried. I added some walnuts to the cake and set it in the oven. It would be done just in time for dessert.

When Mae saw the cake, she jumped up and down. "It smells like Mama!" she exclaimed.

"It's Mama's carrot cake," I said with pride.

After our meal I placed the cake in the center of the table, displaying it for Papa and Mae. They both ate several pieces, commenting on how good it tasted.

"It is as good as your mother's cake," Papa said, "maybe better."

I felt myself flush with joy.

"I liked her johnnycake best," Mae said with a thoughtful look on her face. "But carrot cake is good, too."

"What did you like best about Mama?" I asked Papa.

He looked down a moment as if thinking. When he looked up, his eyes were moist.

"Everything," he said.

Bagpipes and Ribbons

"Caledonia is celebrating its twenty-fifth anniversary next month," I told Mae as I examined the garden. "There will be a parade and fireworks and prizes for the best vegetables."

"What are you going to enter?" Mae asked.

"Nothing." I shook my head in dismay. I'd worked harder than ever to save Mama's garden from blight and the sun's wilting rays. But with all my attention it still didn't return to its original lush state.

"Evie and Mae." Aunt Flo called to us with cool mugs of lemonade. "The garden is coming back nicely," she said as she handed us our drinks.

I frowned. "It isn't good enough. I was hoping to win a ribbon for Mama's squash at the Caledonia fair."

Aunt Flo crossed her arms. "It would be a challenge for anyone to revive it after what it's been through."

I met her eyes. "It would take a miracle, wouldn't it?"

Aunt Flo hesitated. "Not a miracle, but perhaps more work than a young girl can do on her own."

I looked down at my hands, which had turned as brown as the bark of the old walnut tree. I was almost ready to give up. School would resume in just two weeks, and I would have less time to tend to the garden. Our squash had always turned a deep forest green, but the five plants that had blossomed on each of the six small hills were small and sickly looking.

"I've done everything I could do," I admitted. "But the squash just isn't growing like it should."

"I see," she replied as she studied the plants.

"And I wanted our supply to take us through the winter this year," I added with a sigh.

"Have you tried thinning out the hills?" Aunt Flo asked.

"No." I hadn't thought of that. "We usually leave five or six plants on each mound," I replied.

"Since the young plants are established, you should thin each hill to two or three plants and increase the distance between each to about eight feet. That will allow more room for growth. Then hoe and cultivate the hills."

"I guess I can try that," I said as the cicadas buzzed in the distance, a sure sign that summer would be ending soon.

School was canceled the day of the Caledonia fair. Papa woke up in a good mood.

"It has become a prosperous year after all," Papa said at breakfast that early September morn. "The extra acres I planted made up for the storm damage. And the vegetable garden flourished under Evie's excellent care."

"Except for the beans," I said. "They never did return. But the potatoes made up for it." I turned to Aunt Flo. "Your idea worked. The squash has shown the most improvement."

"Enough to earn a ribbon today at the fair?" Aunt Flo asked.

"Perhaps," I replied as a glint of hope filled my chest.

After we cleaned up the breakfast dishes we headed out. I carried several of Mama's best-looking squash in a basket in the back of the wagon. Aunt Flo balanced a blueberry pie on her lap for the dessert table.

"I want to see the Boys in Blue," Mae said, worried that we would miss the parade because the streets were so full of wagons. We parked a half mile from town and walked with all the country folk, each of them carrying baskets of food and vegetables for judging.

"Oh, dear," Aunt Flo said when she saw the tables filled with more blueberry pies than we could count.

"None of them tastes as good as yours," Papa reassured her.

I checked in the squash and received a number, which identified my vegetables. Then I joined Papa and Aunt Flo and Mae at the parade.

We cheered at the procession of Caledonia's war heroes and a brigade of Scottish bagpipe players dressed in tartan plaid. We listened to the mayor's speech as he told of the town's founding. Then we returned to the dessert table, where more than forty different kinds of cake awaited us, in addition to the pie and fresh watermelon.

There were contests of all kinds, from corn shelling to wood splitting. Papa laughed more in one day than he had all year. Aunt Flo contributed to a celebration quilt in progress. I took Mae and left to wander back to the table where the vegetables were being judged.

Would I even know my own squash? I wondered as I saw four long tables heaped with healthy green and gold vegetables. I followed the tables, searching for number fifty-nine.

"It should be on the third table," I told Mae. "Number fifty-nine." We continued searching for my number.

"Is it on that table, Evie?" Mae pointed at the last table, filled with vegetables decorated with colorful ribbons.

I read the numbers on the squash. The third squash with a white ribbon looked familiar.

"Fifty-nine," I said aloud, and checked my ticket to make sure I had the correct number. "I took third place. I won a ribbon!" Mae and I jumped up and down, squealing with delight.

We hurried back to tell Aunt Flo, who embraced me in a huge hug. "I had my suspicions all along that you'd win."

"Thanks, Aunt Flo," I said, enjoying the moment and the hug more than I dared admit. Papa and Mae and Aunt Flo and I celebrated as we ate a Scottish dinner, which included my favorite dish, black pudding.

Later the townspeople spread their blankets near the park, in anticipation of the fireworks. I met

up with Edward, who had won a ribbon at the spelling bee.

"How do you like your aunt?" Edward asked me as
we walked to the park. Gertie and Rita, his older sisters, walked in front of us. I saw them look back and
giggle, then whisper to each other.

"I don't know." I shrugged, not wanting to admit
how much I had gotten used to the sound of Aunt
Flo's humming each morning, how I enjoyed her
jovial teasing with Papa. She had a way about her that
seemed harsh but sort of kind at the same time. She
would yell at Papa when he swore in German, then
turn and smile at us as though she had just made a joke.

I thought of how she didn't tell Papa on me for
spilling the butter. She helped me with the squash and
canned all the vegetables that I picked from my garden, yet never stepped inside it, as if she understood
that it was still a private place for just Mama and me.
Her big hands gently braided Mae's hair every day,
and even though I often twisted my hair in a bun, I
found myself longing for her touch as well.

"I like her," Edward said quietly. "We're thankful for everything she did when Grandpa died."

"What do you mean?"

"Laying him out so nice and all. My mother says it's a talent."

I hadn't thought of it as a talent before. I remembered how Aunt Flo kept referring to it as a calling.

"Will she do all the shrouding for the county?" Edward asked.

"I'm not sure," I replied, realizing that Aunt Flo could be kept very busy, especially in some of the bigger towns. I'd thought she would just do shrouding for our neighbors and a few townsfolk when needed.

As we watched the fireworks under the night sky, I thought about Aunt Flo. It seemed that the real clue to her shrouding was stored in the wooden box underneath her bed. There was only one way to find out what was in that box.

Stealing the Box

It was past midnight before I dared sneak out of the loft. The wooden steps replied with a soft groan as I crept down to the first floor.

The door to Aunt Flo's room was partly open. I slithered into her room, my belly rubbing against the cold wood, across the braided rug until I was right up against the edge of the bed. The moonlight filtering through a tree outside cast a shadow across the room, but I couldn't see underneath her bed. I poked my hand around and swept it back and forth, hoping to come across the box. My hand hit an object, but as I started to bring it out into the light, I realized it was one of Aunt Flo's shoes.

You should quit, a voice inside tugged at me. Papa would be furious, and Aunt Flo would be angry, too. She had been kind, and it was getting harder to dislike her. But curiosity had the better of me, and my hand kept sweeping until it hit something else. I slowly brought out a square object, fingering the top, recognizing it as the lid of the box.

Suddenly something fell over the side of the bed, slightly brushing my hair. It was Aunt Flo's hand, which now hung carelessly above me, inches from the top of my head. I couldn't back up, so instead I wiggled underneath.

A faint light touched a corner on the other side of the bed, so I inched myself and the box toward it. I tried to hold the box up to the light, but it jingled softly.

Gently I put one hand in the box and the other

one over my mouth in case something inside caused me to scream. I heard a squeaking noise from above as Aunt Flo turned in her sleep. I held my breath as I listened to her breathe softly. I removed my hand from the box and silently placed the lid back on top. Then I slid backward, bringing the box with me, as I made my way to the loft. I knew it was wrong to take Aunt Flo's box, but I couldn't stop myself. I had to know what was inside. I tucked the box under our bed. I would wake before Mae and peek inside with the morning light.

Before I fell asleep, I heard footsteps below and the sound of Mama's rocker. Papa couldn't sleep again even after Aunt Flo had stuffed his pillow with hops. I wondered if Papa found Mama in her rocker just as I found her in the garden. The idea was comforting and lulled me to sleep.

The next morning I overslept, and Aunt Flo had to wake me for school. I pushed the box even farther under my bed before I left and stuffed my winter petticoat in front of it just in case. I hurried off to school, planning to take a good look at the contents of the box immediately after I got home.

The day passed too slowly, with an arithmetic test making it seem even longer. I could barely contain myself as I thought of what awaited me in the loft. I planned how to get rid of Mae so I would have some time alone. I would take my rag dolls outside and let her play with them, even my favorite one that Mama had made.

All my planning was in vain, though, for when I got home, Papa was sitting with Mae in the kitchen.

"Where's Aunt Flo?" I asked.

"She was called to perform a shrouding," Papa replied. "I was just waiting for you to come home so I could get back to the chores. You'll have to finish the wash and prepare supper tonight."

"A shrouding?" My voice jumped an octave. "Where?" I asked in a deliberately normal voice, trying to keep calm.

"The other side of the county. Some new settlers lost their father to an infection. I guess they'll most likely head back east now." Papa shook his head, his eyes full of pity.

A huge knot started to form in my stomach. Aunt Flo surely would have said something to Papa if she couldn't find her box. But Papa acted like nothing was wrong, and he wasn't one to hide his anger. I was bewildered and managed only to stammer, "O-oh," in response.

As soon as Papa left, I turned toward Mae with such intensity that she backed away.

"What did I do?" she asked, cowering behind the table.

"Go outside, Mae!" I yelled. I had to get that box back under Aunt Flo's bed before she returned. My heart raced with fear, and I felt my face grow hot.

Mae scrunched up her face, and I thought she would burst into tears. I forced myself to relax and fixed a smile upon my face. "Nothing is wrong, Mae. I just thought you'd like to go outside and play."

The urgency of my voice must have hit a chord. Mae immediately became contrary. "No, thank you." She skipped around the kitchen to taunt me.

"But Mae, I have work to do inside, cleaning to be done and food to prepare. You have to play outside."

"No, I don't," she answered stubbornly.

I stomped my foot down as I felt the frustration build inside. If she didn't go outside, she'd follow me up to the loft and wonder what I was doing searching under the bed. I couldn't possibly confide in her. Mae's secrets rarely lasted more than five minutes before they poured out of her, and after the butter churn incident I knew she would tell on me. I remembered my rag dolls.

"I'll let you play with my dolls if you go outside."

Even my rag dolls didn't convince Mae. "No," she replied in a defiant voice, as if she knew how much I wanted her to leave.

"Fine," I finally said. "If you stay inside, you have to work. Let's see how good you are at snapping green beans."

Mae considered it for a moment. I knew she hated snapping beans, a job she was always given because it was easy. Finally she shook her head at me. "I won't," she insisted. "I'm going outside to find precious pebbles."

"Stay nearby," I warned her, even though it was hard to contain my glee at finally getting rid of her.

My stomach quivered as I neared the bedroom door. Already my mind was spinning through ideas on how I could keep out of trouble.

If I put the box in a corner under her bed, maybe she'll think she somehow missed it when she was looking. Surely a person could make a mistake like that.

For the first time since I'd come home, my heart felt lighter, and I sensed a newfound hope. The hope turned immediately to horror when I entered my bedroom. On the end of my bed, folded very neatly, I saw my petticoat.

Sickness

The next few hours were the longest of my life. The box was not under my bed. I searched beneath Aunt Flo's bed, but it wasn't there, either. Aunt Flo had the box with her, and she knew that I had stolen it.

I was sorry, more sorry than I'd ever been in my life. I thought of telling Papa what I'd done, but I couldn't seem to find the voice for it. Instead I swept out the kitchen, hung up the wash, and put cabbage on to boil. All the while, I felt like my heart was pulled up into my throat. Soon Aunt Flo would come back and

I'd have to face her and Papa. I didn't even get to see what was in the box. All that for nothing, and I'd be punished for it, too. I fixed supper and Papa came in to eat, commenting on how unusually quiet I was.

"You feeling all right?" he asked.

"Yes, Papa."

"Evie yelled at me," Mae volunteered.

"Perhaps something is bothering Evie," Papa observed.

I looked down and said nothing.

The evening dragged on, and I couldn't concentrate on anything for more than a few moments. I'd stop what I was doing and run to the door if I heard the slightest noise. I wanted a chance to apologize to Aunt Flo in private. But Papa yawned and said we all had better get to bed. I stalled, going as slowly as possible, until Papa finally blew out the lamp. I knew I wouldn't be able to sleep. I twisted and turned until Mae threatened to tell Papa that I was keeping her awake. Later I lay there quietly, wishing Aunt Flo would just come home and get it over with.

The next thing I remembered, I felt someone shaking me. I looked up to see Aunt Flo standing above me, a dim light from outside shining in. It was almost dawn.

"You'd better hurry," she said. "You'll be late for school."

I followed her into the kitchen and noticed that Papa's boots were missing from the back door. He was already out doing chores.

"You were gone a long time last night," I said in as pleasant a voice as I could muster. "I waited up to talk to you."

"There's no time for talk now," she replied curtly. "Your breakfast is on the table. Go now, before you are late."

I got ready and went to school with a heavy feeling in my stomach, like the weight of my morning flapjacks, although I knew it wasn't food that was making me feel this way. Aunt Flo had said nothing to me about the box, and the guilt I felt stayed with me through the day. I mulled over my actions, fearing that Aunt Flo knew my secret and was now telling Papa about it.

I got into trouble twice in class for not paying attention and had my knuckles rapped for the first time ever. But the humiliation of that seemed pale in comparison to what waited for me later.

I dawdled all the way home. Even Edward and his sisters left me behind. I knew Papa would take Aunt Flo's side, and I knew I was wrong to take her box. Finally I decided to face them. I would apologize and take my punishment like the martyrs I'd read about who courageously faced the lions.

When I walked in the door, Papa was waiting for me.

"Aunt Flo is under the weather," he said. "She says it's just a cold, but I sent her to bed. You'll have to make supper tonight." Then he went back out to tend to his chores.

Mae fretted all evening as if she was remembering Mama's sickness again. I worried, too, even though I knew Mama's illness was something much worse.

It's from staying out so late with her shrouding duties,
I thought, and I was filled with a sudden remorse.

I brought Aunt Flo a bowl of potato soup and a
cup of tea.

"Thank you, Evie," she said as she sat up. She
looked pale and worn.

"Aunt Flo," I said softly, "I need to talk to you
about your box." I looked down at the floor,
ashamed.

"My shrouding box is underneath my bed where I
always keep it," she said firmly. "There's no need to
discuss it."

I looked up into her face. I expected to see anger and
disappointment, but all I saw was the determination of
an aunt who seemed to love me in spite of myself.

The next morning Aunt Flo felt better and got up to
fix breakfast, chasing Papa away from the stove.

"I'll stay home and help," I offered.

She shook her head. "I will have none of that. I'm just a little weak. If I stay in bed all day, I'll never get my strength back."

I smiled at her before I left and told her not to overdo it. She patted me on the back.

That day I did my schoolwork with a lighter heart and didn't get into trouble once. I even challenged Edward to a race home after school although he beat me.

Aunt Flo still looked tired that evening but seemed in good spirits, even telling us stories from her time spent in the Dakotas. She told us how people there built their sod homes at the corner of their land so they could be next to each other through the lonely, hard winters. She also boasted of the tough women on the prairie, of one woman who could shoot the skin off a snake from fifty yards.

Then she talked about growing up with Papa. She spoke of losing two brothers to typhoid on the ship to America, brothers Papa never met.

"One was named Hans," she said. "When my mother had another son in America, she named him after the son who'd died."

"Do you remember much about him?" I asked.

"No," she replied. "I was young. I was just five."

I looked over at Mae, who was also five years old. Would *she* remember Mama?

Another Shrouding

I had just fallen asleep when a loud pounding awoke me. I saw Papa pull up his suspenders as he hurried toward the door. Aunt Flo was close behind him carrying a lantern, and I trailed them both. Mae didn't even wake up. I turned to speak to Aunt Flo, but she quietly shushed me as Papa went to see who was there.

Papa opened the door. I didn't recognize the man standing outside, but he had a distraught look on his face and wrung a handkerchief back and forth between his hands.

"Howdy, Mr. Paulson," Papa said, stepping back and motioning him inside. I stood huddled with Aunt Flo against the wall.

"Sorry to bother you at this time of night, Mr. Mennen. But we are in need of your sister's services. We've had a death in the family."

Papa patted the man on the shoulder and looked back at Aunt Flo. Her face was still flush with cold.

"My sister is ill," he told the man.

The man kept talking. "It's my eldest daughter. She was carrying our grandson. Had a terrible hard time delivering him. The doctor finally was able to pull the baby out, but it was just too hard on Clara. The doctor spent most of the evening with her. We lost her." He choked on those last words.

"I will go," Aunt Flo said, then hurried to her room to change.

Papa turned to me. "She isn't feeling well, Evie." He looked worried. "Aunt Flo may need help."

I stared at Papa, not understanding what he was asking.

"Evie, you will go with her."

My eyes opened wide and my throat tightened. "But I don't know anything about shrouding, Papa."

"Just do what she tells you."

I hesitated. "What if I can't, Papa?"

He put his hands on my shoulders. "Just think of all Aunt Flo has done for us. That will help you find the courage."

I followed Aunt Flo, who was getting ready. I brought out the box from under the bed and held it up to her.

"Papa would like me to come with you."

Aunt Flo was fastening her dress, but she stopped and stared at me, her eyes wide in disbelief. "I don't think that is a good idea, Evie."

"I want to help," I insisted.

She waved me away with her hand. "You are young, Evie. You should not be concerned with this."

"How old were you when your grandmother taught you?"

She looked thoughtful for a moment. "I was about your age when I first went with my *Oma*. But this is different."

"Please, Aunt Flo. I won't be in the way."

Aunt Flo studied my face, puzzled. "Are you certain you want to go?"

"Yes," I said, determined now to convince her.

Aunt Flo hesitated. "All right, but you must be very quiet and not ask questions."

Then I did something I didn't expect to do. I gave Aunt Flo a hug.

"I won't," I said even as I wondered what I had gotten myself into. "I promise."

Shrouding Duties

I snuggled beneath a gray, tattered blanket in the back of Mr. Paulson's wagon, headed for the other side of the county. The night was cool, but Aunt Flo didn't seem to notice. She sat up straight, staring ahead onto the dark road; the lantern sitting next to her transformed the bushes and trees into strange shapes. Poor Mr. Paulson spoke quietly to Aunt Flo every once in a while.

"She was our first child," he said more than once.

I was almost asleep when the wagon slowly turned

down a tree-lined path, blocking off even the light of the moon to guide us. My teeth chattered, although I didn't know if it was from the cold or fear of what might lie ahead. My stomach felt nervous.

The Paulsons lived in a small home surrounded by trees, about a half mile off the road. The sound of a stream broke the silence of the night, and the horses whinnied a greeting that announced our presence. A small light flickered in the window, and I saw the door open slightly as we drew near. Mrs. Paulson greeted us at the door with red eyes.

As we entered, we heard a cry coming from a darkened corner near the fire. Mrs. Paulson hurried over to a bassinet and picked up a baby tightly wrapped in blankets.

"God spared our grandson," she said quietly. I looked at the tiny infant. A patch of light hair crowned his little head. My heart filled with sympathy for him. He squirmed restlessly, and I wondered if he sensed his mother's death.

Mrs. Paulson offered us some tea to warm up.

"Perhaps later," Aunt Flo said. "Best we tend to our duties first."

Mrs. Paulson led us to a bedroom at the back of the house where a young man with dark hair and eyes was keeping a vigil near the figure on the bed. He looked to be about eighteen years old. Aunt Flo paused outside the bedroom door and looked at me.

"Do you want to stay out here, Evie?"

I shook my head. "No," I replied, my voice barely a whisper. My stomach rumbled and I felt lightheaded, but still I said, "I want to help."

Aunt Flo offered her condolences to the young man and then quietly instructed him to fetch her a long board. He left in a trance, as though unaware of what he was doing.

Aunt Flo took the basin of water and the soap that was next to the bed and laid a cloth and towel beside it. She opened the box and brought out a brush and a round container that held some powder. Finally she took out two pennies, a bag containing a mixture of herbs and spices, and one of the forked twigs.

When the man returned with the board, she draped a pretty white sheet on top. Next she helped him position the woman on it. Then she told him to go fetch some old pieces of cloth.

He came back a minute later with some small linens.

"Go now, rest and see your new son," Aunt Flo told him. "I'll take care of your wife."

He left, still in a stupor, but his eyes flickered and he thanked Aunt Flo.

I still hadn't looked at the woman on the bed. My eyes had stayed fixed upon Aunt Flo and the assortment of items before her.

Aunt Flo moved quickly now, removing the woman's gown. Taking a cloth, she carefully washed the woman's body, mixing the sweet-smelling herbs and spices into the water. Then she washed her hair with some soap and water. Afterward she took a lavender dress with a high lace collar that was hanging in the corner and placed it on the woman.

Next Aunt Flo put stockings and shoes on the woman and started to comb her blond hair. Aunt Flo had such a natural way about her, I had to keep reminding myself that the woman was dead.

I made myself look at the woman's hands and arms. My eyes moved to her hair, so pretty and thick, with long golden waves. Finally, ever so slowly, my eyes came to rest on her face. She had a beautiful, small face, and a look of peace showed upon it. Her eyes were partly closed.

Aunt Flo moved gracefully as she picked up the coins. *That's what rattled in the box,* I thought. She closed both eyelids, placing a penny on each one, and said quietly, "The coins keep the eyes shut."

I hadn't moved since I entered the room. "Hand me the twig, Evie," Aunt Flo asked. Fear had frozen me to one spot on the floor, and I thought I would faint if I budged an inch. But my feet walked on their own, and somehow I handed the twig to Aunt Flo.

She took the forked twig and propped it underneath the woman's chin, inserting it so that the twig was covered under her lace collar. "It holds the head up and keeps the mouth closed," she said as she straightened the collar over it.

Aunt Flo moistened several cloths in camphor and covered the woman's arms and hands with them.

"This keeps the skin white. Otherwise it turns an ashen color," Aunt Flo explained. "I'll remove the cloths in the morning before the service."

Finally Aunt Flo took the powder and fluffed it on the woman's face.

"The dark powder covers the pale mask of death," she said.

Aunt Flo took a cloth dipped in some dried rose petals and put a pinch on each cheek. Then she placed a pillow underneath the head of the woman and stepped back, a look of quiet fulfillment on her face.

I spoke for the first time. "She appears as if she's asleep."

"Yes." Aunt Flo nodded. "She is at peace." She sat down on a rocking chair next to the bed and picked up a Bible. "Now we sit and wait."

"For what?"

"For morning. Someone needs to sit up with the body throughout the night. Look, it is almost dawn now."

The room suddenly seemed very quiet. Aunt Flo rocked slowly back and forth, reading from the Bible, her lips forming the words as she read. Her face was still flushed, but she didn't seem ill. I slowly inched myself toward the corner, where I slouched down, my eyes still on the woman in the center of the room. Aunt Flo and I and death, alone together, the three of us.

I sat there another hour with Aunt Flo, who rocked and read the time away. My body began to relax, and I sank farther down in the corner. I looked at the box on the floor next to Aunt Flo. There were only a few coins and twigs, some powder and herbs and spices, and dried rose petals. And there was Aunt Flo, who made death less painful for the grieving relatives. As I watched Aunt Flo rock, I had to strain to keep my eyes from closing.

❧

Bam, bam, bam! I quickly woke to the sound of pounding and hurried toward the window. In the faint first glow of the day, I saw Mr. Paulson building a coffin for Clara. I looked at his daughter on the board, who seemed more of a girl than a woman. Her long silky hair glistened in the morning light.

Then I started to cry.

Aunt Flo looked at me and opened her arms. I ran to her and sat on her lap. Her big arms wrapped around me tightly.

"It is good to cry," Aunt Flo said. "Let it out, Evie. Let the sorrow go."

It seemed like I sobbed forever, until there was nothing left inside me. It was the first time I'd cried since Mama's death. When I couldn't cry any longer, exhaustion set in and I soon nodded off to sleep in Aunt Flo's arms.

The Gift of Life

Was it a dream? I jumped out of bed and ran to the kitchen. Mae sat at the table, eating hot porridge, her favorite. She slurped a spoonful into her mouth and smiled when she noticed me standing there.

"Evie is a sleepyhead," she taunted me. I turned without answering her taunt. The sun was already halfway across the kitchen floor, which meant I had slept late again.

"Where are Papa and Aunt Flo?"

"Papa is feeding the sheep. Aunt Flo is taking care of the garden because you're a sleepyhead." I stood still for so long that Mae finally asked, "Evie, are you sick?"

I didn't answer her. I ran out the door toward the garden. Before I reached it, I heard a humming sound coming from the far side. Aunt Flo was on her knees, pulling the weeds from the white flowers of the wild boneset I'd planted around one edge of the garden. Only a few melons and a couple of stalks of corn with husks lingered in the Indian summer.

I stopped running and ducked behind a tree as I watched her. Her face seemed to radiate the sun as she hummed a German song that I recalled from before. Suddenly my spirit lifted, as if the stone that had been dragging me down had broken apart into little pieces and crumbled away.

The following day another caller came to our house. It was William Friedrich, whose wife, Sophie, was due to have a baby.

"Oh, no," I whispered to myself when I saw his wagon turn up our mud drive. "Poor Sophie has died. Or is it her baby that's died?" I remembered Sophie from school, although she had been years ahead of me in her studies.

Papa was in the barn, feeding the animals, so Aunt Flo went outside to talk to William. After a couple of minutes, she returned and grabbed her shawl.

"Tell your father that I have gone with Mr. Friedrich and should not be back too late. You watch Mae and start the potatoes boiling if I don't get home by suppertime."

"Aunt Flo, you forgot your box."

"I don't need it, Evie. Mr. Friedrich has asked me to help deliver their baby. The doctor is busy treating Mr. Stein's inflammation."

"So no one has died?"

"No, Evie. God willing, I will help deliver a healthy child."

My mouth dropped open. "You know how to do that?"

"Yes, I've helped many times." She winked at me and added, "It is good to see the beginning of life and not just the end."

I watched Aunt Flo leave, the wagon turning toward town, and I marveled at all she knew. I hadn't been very kind to her, and still she took care of Mae and Papa and me.

I waited anxiously for Aunt Flo to come home to share news of Sophie's baby. I put the potatoes on to boil, shook out all the rugs, and swept the parlor floor. Then I sat at the table and did my school lessons.

I also made a funeral card that I planned to put on the grave of Mr. Paulson's daughter who was buried in the cemetery next to town. I thought of how there would be two births in one week and how their children would someday go to school together, maybe even become friends. By the time Papa came inside, I was exhausted.

"How much time does it take to deliver a baby?" I asked Papa.

He shook his head. "There's no set amount, but you took so long, I corded two loads of wood and still had time to spare."

When the wagon finally turned up our drive, I ran outside to greet Aunt Flo. "Is the baby all right?"

"*Ja.*" Aunt Flo nodded. "It is a healthy baby girl."

"A girl," I repeated.

"They have named her Constance, after Mrs. Friedrich's mother."

"When I have a daughter, I will name her Rose, after my mother," I said.

Aunt Flo frowned, but her voice was light. "It's a nice thought, but don't be in a rush to marry. Think of all you need to learn first."

Then she got down from the wagon and put her hand on my shoulder. "For instance, you can start by helping me cook up a mustard plaster for chest colds."

"Phew." I could only cover my nose at the thought.

A Shrouding Assistant

New settlers often left after spending one winter in Minnesota. Papa prided himself on surviving the winters, but this year we thought it would never end. Storms continued to pile snow upon the garden, burying any visible signs that it ever existed, stopping only long enough for us to dig our way out before beginning the cycle all over again. The weather made it almost impossible for Aunt Flo to do any shrouding.

During the cold, gray days, I thought more and more about her calling. I remembered the night when I went with Aunt Flo to the Paulsons' and how my opinion of laying out the dead had changed since then. I was afraid to ask the question that burned inside me. It took me a good part of the winter to get up the nerve.

I finally posed the question on a dreary day as I sat near the stove and practiced knitting, with one long line of white yarn stretching down to the floor by my feet. Aunt Flo stood nearby, mixing a batch of biscuits on the table, her thick hands pushing the flour into the mix.

"How does a person know if she should be a shrouding woman?" I asked.

"I don't really know," she replied. "I followed in my mother's footsteps. It seemed the natural thing to do." Aunt Flo looked down at my stitches. "They need to be closer together," she advised me.

"How did you decide that you were that type of person?" I asked as I accidentally dropped a stitch off my needle.

"It is something you know as you grow older."

"But what if you are mistaken?"

"You will know that, also, with time." She stopped mixing the biscuits and looked at me with curious eyes. "Why do you ask so many questions about it?"

"I want to learn."

"There is only one way to learn." She leaned over. "I am in need of an assistant."

"Oh, no. Not me." I shook my head.

"Why not?"

"I'm not sure I could do it," I admitted.

She glanced sideways at me, a half smile on her lips. "I think otherwise." She reached up and brushed a hair from her face with her floury hand. "You consider it awhile. You will certainly have all your questions answered that way."

I mulled over her offer. Aunt Flo didn't give false praise. If she said that I could do it, then she honestly felt that way. If I helped her, I would certainly learn more about shrouding.

After a week of pondering back and forth like a see-saw, I decided to satisfy my curiosity.

"I'm ready to become your assistant," I announced to her after dinner.

"You must watch first," she said. "Watch and learn. Then you can help." She sighed. "God willing, I won't be called this winter."

But less than a week later, a young Scot came to fetch her. His father had fallen through the ice on their pond. I accompanied Aunt Flo to the shrouding and watched, staying out of the way while she worked her simple magic.

In the middle of January, Aunt Flo was called to another shrouding, and this time she allowed me to assist her a bit from the side. In a cradle I saw a baby boy who looked like a little doll, with a porcelain face and long lashes. I didn't dread looking upon him, though. I handed Aunt Flo her coins, mixed the herbs and spices into the water, and gave her the delicate lace-trimmed gown to dress the baby. The baby's mother held the small bundle one more time before he was laid into a miniature coffin.

Two weeks later an old woman died. Her small, shriveled body looked to be near a hundred years old. I recited Scripture from the Bible as the woman's relatives crowded around the small cabin. This pleased many of the folks who couldn't read. I saw the comfort it gave them as they bowed their heads, a calm look coming upon their faces. Aunt Flo said that I had a natural compassion, something that couldn't be taught.

Maybe I do have a talent, I thought.

I watched Aunt Flo carefully, noting how she put a smattering of rose petal dust on the woman's cheeks and her forehead. I studied her moves as she folded the hands in a certain way and set the sticks at a specific spot under her chin.

Papa made Aunt Flo a "cooling-down board" to lay the bodies on while she prepared them for burial, but it wasn't long enough for tall people. The fourth shrouding I attended was for a tall German farmer.

His relatives had to take down a door to use in place of the board.

Aunt Flo started to make a name for herself. It wasn't just the townsfolk and neighbors who visited. People from all over the county called upon her to do the shrouding duties. Sometimes they paid her with food or small gifts, but mostly Aunt Flo refused payment. She said her work was a gift from God and therefore should be offered up to God. I now understood what Edward meant when he said that it was a fine talent.

By the following March, I was a few months shy of twelve and Papa noticed a change in me.

"You are growing into a young woman," he commented as he polished his boots and nailed a loose heel back into place. This was the second time the heel had come loose and Papa had returned from the barn with wet feet.

"Your mama would be proud of you for helping Aunt Flo and especially for all your work in the garden."

I nodded and looked out the window at the snow-covered garden.

"This year the garden will be different," I told Papa.

He looked up from his polishing. "How's that?"

"I don't think Mama wants me to work it alone. There's more than one person can handle."

"Oh, yes," he replied, and a faint smile crossed his lips.

A New Shrouding Woman

With the spring rains came a new beginning.

"Aunt Flo, hurry," I said as I rushed her outside one sunny morning. "I have something to show you."

"What is it?" she asked, her voice expecting the worst.

I took her arm and guided her to the spot. There, on the large shriveled corn plant left from last year's crop, I had tied a pink ribbon.

"What is this?" Aunt Flo raised her eyebrows, a look of bewilderment on her face.

"It's a gift for you."

"You're giving me your garden?" Aunt Flo stared at me for a long second, then her eyes became misty. "This is the garden your mother gave you. You cannot give it away."

"I want to give it to you."

She shook her head. "But why?"

"So that I can help you with it like I helped Mama."

Aunt Flo embraced me tightly. I hugged her back. Aunt Flo wasn't the same as Mama, but she didn't try to be. I knew that Papa missed Mama. Maybe Papa didn't need Aunt Flo just to take care of us. Maybe he needed her to take care of him for a while, too.

That thought seemed to grow on me until I was certain of it. Even though Papa was still sad, he wasn't as sad as before. He started each day with a smile on his face, and I heard the rocking chair less often at night.

In a few weeks' time, Aunt Flo and Mae and I decided
to plant a huge garden. We tilled additional land and
mixed manure into the soil. We separated the flower
seeds that we had dried out last fall to form a border.
The ground cherries were already sprouting amid the
wet, cold soil. Aunt Flo and I created a special herb
section where we would grow shrouding and medicinal plants like onion, thyme, basil, chamomile, and
germander, as well as lily of the valley for color and
dye. We would raise flax to spin into linen for our pet-
ticoats. Papa put in a cottonwood tree off to the side.

Mae and I mapped out just how our garden would
look. We scouted out flat white rocks to use for a
walkway. Papa made a small wooden bench to set in
the middle. We even planted scores of lilies in memory of Mama. I couldn't help but think that it would
be the greatest garden in the county. Papa said it was a
work of art.

The prairie created its own garden with a canvas of
tall green grasses and colorful wildflowers like the

black-eyed Susan, whose dark center peeks out from its bright yellow petals.

I had come home from school, eager to gather a bouquet of scented flowers, when I saw Papa waiting for me with the horses hitched to the wagon.

"Aunt Flo left to do a shrouding on the other side of the county this morning, and she won't be back for another day and a half," he announced. "But a child died of pneumonia while traveling with her family. They would like someone to prepare her for burial even though they won't have much time, as they still have a long travel ahead of them." He paused and looked at me.

Papa cleared his throat before he spoke again. "I told them you would do it, Evie."

"But I'm not a shrouding woman," I objected. "I just help Aunt Flo."

"If you don't do it, who will?" Papa asked.

I hesitated. "You said it is a girl?"

Papa nodded. "About three years old."

I turned and went inside to find some of Aunt Flo's ointments and powders, a brush and some coins, all of which I rolled into a handkerchief. I grabbed my Bible. Then I left with Papa.

Several miles south of town we spotted two dusty wagons packed full of furniture and provisions. At the side of the wagons a man, a woman, and three small children were gathered around a figure laid out on a blanket. The children were clinging to their mother's skirt as she wept above them. The man's face held a look of shock and remorse, as if he had failed to keep his daughter safe. I glanced down at the child. Her hair was blond and her features fair.

My throat tightened and a sudden fear crept upward. I was too young to do this.

"What's her name?" I asked.

"Mary Elizabeth," the woman answered.

I took the mother's hand. "What dress would you like her to be buried in?" I asked her gently.

Tears filled her eyes. "Her favorite is a white frock I made last Christmas. I'll get it."

She fetched the frock, and the family left me to tend to my duties. I unwrapped the handkerchief and carefully took out each item. There wasn't time to wash the child's hair, so I took a damp cloth and sponged her face. "She has brown eyes like me," I said as I fought back my own tears. "Aunt Flo, why aren't you here?"

I struggled as I thought of Mary Elizabeth's family, who were counting on me to help them through this time.

I concentrated on what I had learned and tried to imagine Aunt Flo close by. I removed Mary Elizabeth's gown and put on her dress. I brushed out her tangled hair. Then I used my fingers to apply powder to her skin, rubbing it in as naturally as I could. I closed her eyes and placed a coin on each one. I took the ointments and smoothed an especially fragrant one around her neck, using a forked twig to prop up her small face. When I was finished, I looked down at her. I didn't fight the tears that filled my eyes.

"She deserved better than this," I quietly cried. "She should have had an experienced woman lay her out instead of me."

I opened my Bible and recited several verses for the family before they buried the child under a maple tree next to the road. Then they marked her grave with a wooden cross that had her name and birth date.

Before they left, Mary Elizabeth's mother took out a small shell on a dainty chain. "Mary Elizabeth picked this up on the beach along the Atlantic shore. I know that she would like you to have it," she said as she placed the shell in my hand. "We will remember your kindness always. Thank you."

The Tradition

Sunday, after service, we visited the cemetery where Mama was buried. Papa picked out the long grass crowding up from the edge of the stone cross that marked her grave. Mae sprinkled timothy clover around the sides. Aunt Flo read a Scripture passage from the Bible.

"I miss you, Mama," I whispered, bowing my head. I knelt down to place a bouquet of lilies on her grave. When I looked up and squinted into the sun, there, in the distance, was an animal staring at me from the shadows of a tall pine. It looked like a fox. And I could have sworn I saw a white tip on its ear.

Several months later I sat alone on the bench in the middle of our garden. It was a quiet time in the late afternoon. Mae was asleep under the cottonwood tree, and Aunt Flo was busy in the kitchen. Papa was out in the fields. I was surrounded by the scent of herbs combined with Mama's lilies.

It had been a year since Aunt Flo came into our lives, just a little more than a year since Mama died. I looked up and saw Mama's image, hazy in the afternoon sun, bending over the cabbage, her bonnet catching the light just so. I rubbed my eyes and realized it was a tree branch catching the shadows and playing tricks on me. Her bonnet was the foxglove and purple verbena bending in the breeze. But Mama was here. I could feel her presence just as I could feel the wind on my face. She was part of this garden, just like Aunt Flo was now part of the garden and Mae and Papa and me, too.

I fingered the shell that I wore; I hadn't taken it off since Mary Elizabeth's mother gave it to me. As I sat there, I realized how much shrouding was like gardening, each offering a bit of peace for the living and the dead. Mama said the earth brings forth life. Aunt Flo said the earth takes back life. Both of them were right.

Author's Note

My great-grandmother grew up near the Crooked Creek Valley in Saratoga, Minnesota. "Little Grandma" often told stories of her large family, of getting a whipping when she wandered too far from home, and of the death of her five-year-old daughter. The greatest discovery in my research was the diary of my great-great-grandmother Rachel Cornelius, whose record of daily life in Caledonia in the 1870s helped me understand the everyday concerns that Evie would have faced.

The Crooked Creek Valley attracted pioneers from Scotland, Germany, and Norway. The rich area provided an abundance of wild turkey and fish. Blueberries and raspberries were plentiful in the summer. The people of Caledonia took pride in the fact that their town was progressive and had been founded five years before Minnesota became a state.

The *Minnesota Farmer's Diaries* and the journal of pioneer Dave Wood helped me understand the difficult life of a farmer and his dependence on weather. But those journals also recount that pioneers still found time for pleasure and church, and I wanted Evie's story to reflect that as well.

I first read about shrouding women while sitting in a hospital room as my son recovered from surgery. At the time, I was somewhat shocked by the idea, but I was equally fascinated. While not much is written about the tradition, it is mentioned in many prairie journals and appeared to be a common practice.

Up until the late 1800s, when a person died, people called upon a "shrouding woman" or "layer out of the dead" to prepare the body for burial (or if a shrouder wasn't available, a kind female neighbor offered the service). Most often a casket was built by a family member. There were no funeral homes or undertakers, so providing for the dead was a part of everyday life for the pioneers.

Viewing of the body took place at home in the parlor. Families didn't leave the dead unattended because of superstition, rats and other animals, and the slight hope that the deceased would come back to life. Occasionally a person would start breathing again *before* burial. This was rare but caused some mourners to tie a string around the finger of the deceased that connected to a bell aboveground, in case of premature burial.

The word *shrouding* comes from *shroud,* a cloth wrapped around a body for burial in ancient times. The custom of women preparing bodies for burial can be traced back to the time of Jesus. The art of laying out the dead was passed down from one generation to the next. Most shrouding women were not paid but were treated as honored members of the community for performing this "last sacred duty to the dead."

Georgeanne Rundblad, professor of sociology at Illinois Wesleyan University, studied the tradition of shrouding and shared her findings with me. Many women, like Martha Ballard who lived in New England in the late 1700s, combined their laying-out duties with those of a midwife. Other women, like Willie Mae Cartwright's mother who lived in the South in the late 1800s, were a select few who performed only the tasks of shrouding. Like Evie, young Willie Mae accompanied her mother on several occasions and served as an assistant. Girls also took on the duty of sewing mourning pictures of family members who had died, much like Evie's needlework memorial.

During the Civil War, the technology of embalming was developed, and funeral preparation turned into a profitable business. In a field that was once dominated by women, laying out of the dead quickly became a male occupation, and women were suddenly seen as frail and not fit for this line of work; however, the rural parts of the country still continued the ritual for many years. *The Shrouding Woman* gives voice to a rich tradition that has been overlooked in this century, a tradition whose place in history is significant.